GW01393228

THE BEATLES

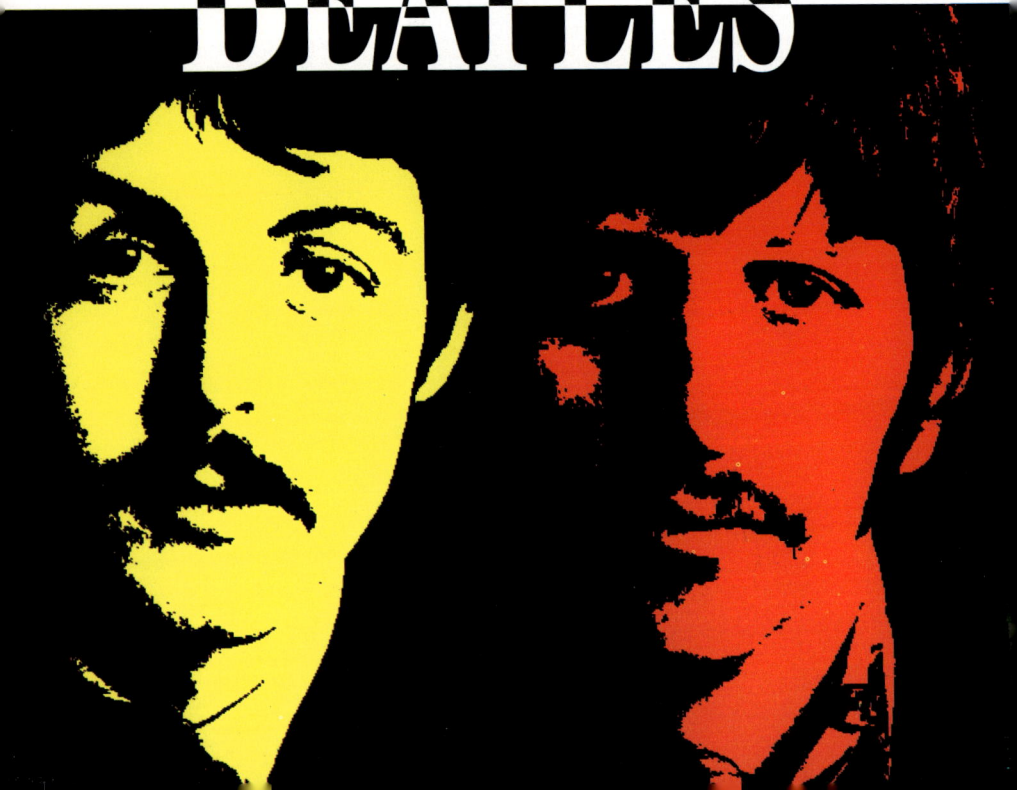

THE BEATLES

ORION

JON EWING

AN ORION PAPERBACK

This is a Carlton Book

First published in Great Britain in 1994 by Orion Books Ltd, Orion House,
5 Upper St Martin's Lane, London, WC2H 9EA.

Text and design © 1994 Carlton Books Ltd
CD Guide format © 1994 Carlton Books Ltd

A CIP catalogue record for this book is available from the British Library.

ISBN 1 85797 928 1

Edited, designed and typeset by Archetype Ltd.
Printed in Italy

THE AUTHOR
Jon Ewing is a freelance writer. His contributions have included work for film,
music and computer game magazines.

CONTENTS

INTRODUCTION

In the very beginning, the Sixties didn't "swing", and even rebel-rousers like Elvis Presley were starting to sound old hat. If you tuned in to the main—and apart from unlicensed pirate stations, only—pop music outlet on UK radio on a drizzly Sunday afternoon, Alan Freeman's *Pick Of The Pops*, on BBC Radio, you would have been crying out for something new, something fresh… anything different.

Then, in early 1963, four young musicians wearing uniform grey suits with chopped lapels and floppy fringes arrived in the world of showbiz in a blaze of publicity, fresh from Liverpool on the banks of the river Mersey.

"You have to be a real sour square not to love the nutty, noisy, happy, handsome Beatles," said the *Daily Mirror*. "If they don't sweep your blues away—brother, you're a lost cause. If they don't put a beat in your feet—sister, you're not living." First 'Please Please Me' and then 'She Loves You' hijacked the airwaves in a explosion of unprecedented popularity. From the lower-middle class suburbs of an unfashionable north-western English city, John, Paul, George and Ringo rode on a wave of raucous yet harmonious songs that crashed down chaotically all over the world.

It seemed as though the Beatles had made it overnight, but looking back on their journey to the top of the world's charts, the road had been long and winding, with thousands of hours spent in seedy nightclubs, playing cheap guitars and dressed in sweaty leathers. In those years, two of the outstanding songwriters of pop music history, John Lennon and Paul McCartney, had learned their trade together. All they ever wanted was to be famous.

Pop music gave the Beatles everything. For three years, the world's media echoed in celebration of Beatlemania, offering immortality on a silver platter to the Fab Four from Liverpool. But they paid the price, hidden by day from their fans, living a mad whirlwind of locked hotel rooms, limousines and one-night stands before howling masses. They became too successful to enjoy it all.

The Beatles' success made British groups the

Seven years, 11 albums: the four Beatles

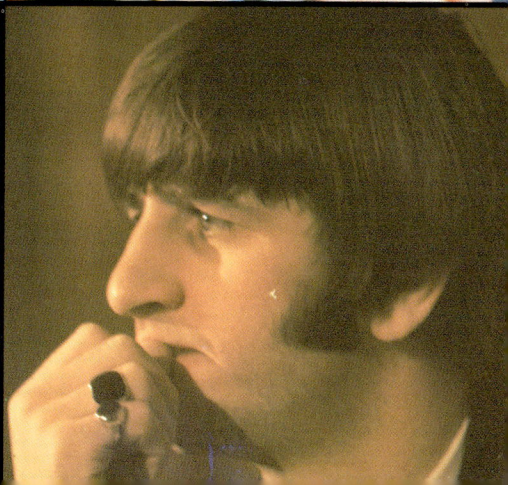

"The Beatles are wacky. They wear their hair like a mop—but it's WASHED, it's super-clean. So is their fresh young act."
Daily Mirror, 1963

The Fab Four from Liverpool had conquered the world as they headlined their 1965 Christmas Show on British television.

internationally most sought after, their home town of Liverpool the world's capital of a new sound and London the centre of every new fashion and youth trend.

Britain was swinging, and for a whole generation of post-war baby boomers, replete with cash in their pockets in a way their forebears had never enjoyed, with free access to university educations and exposed to a flood of new ideas about making love, not war, awareness of the continuing hypocrisy of old-world politics and religion became a catalyst for a cultural revolution. Caught up in this revolution were four visionary young men: the Beatles were artists of the new renaissance, and *Sergeant Pepper's Lonely Hearts Club Band* would be their masterpiece.

It is impossible to estimate the influence of the Beatles' music. Their legacy is far more than a stunning list of million-selling singles and chart-topping albums. They changed the face of popular music by touching it with their genius. More than a quarter of a century after their split, the Beatles are still the world's most famous band.

DOWN PENNY LANE

Few bands spring into instant existence—the construction of a working group is usually one of trial and error, and the Beatles too, went through many trials and made innumerable errors on their way to the top. And in every band there always seems to be one or two members who are core to its growth and success.

Somewhere a dream comes into it, and somewhere ambition as well. With the Beatles, it was John Lennon who was the dreamer, Paul McCartney the ambitious one—but both dreamed of musical success and the destiny of realizing their talent.

Lennon's grandfather, Jack, was born in Dublin, Ireland, and spent most of his life as the singer with a group of travelling minstrels in the USA. In later life he returned to England and had a son named Alfred, who was orphaned when Jack died in 1921.

Alfred (Freddy) Lennon was an itinerant. After leaving his orphanage at 15 he had a string of unambitious jobs before signing up with the merchant navy. He met a young girl called Julia Stanley, who he visited every time his ship docked in Liverpool. They were married there at Mount Pleasant Register Office on December 3, 1938. On October 9, 1940, Julia gave birth to a

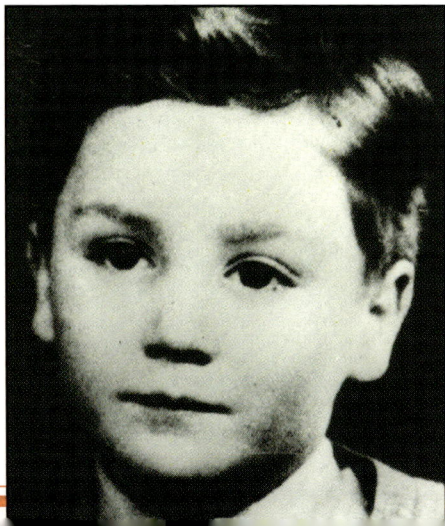

At five, John Lennon was sent to live with his Aunt Mimi in a pleasant Liverpool suburb.

son she named John Winston Lennon. Freddy was nowhere to be found—he had jumped ship in New York. WWII was raging, and for his desertion he ended up in a British military prison in North Africa.

Julia was an attractive young woman, and in 1945 she moved in with a waiter from a Liverpool hotel. He had kids of his own, so her sister, Mimi, took the five-year-old John in o her home—Mendips, in Menlove Avenue, Woolton, a district of Liverpool. Lennon remembered it as a pleasant, suburban area with "doctors and lawyers and that ilk living around". Mimi and her husband, George, who had no children, brought the young boy up as if he were their own son.

"Both Julia and Fred wanted me to adopt him," said Mimi, "I've got letters from them saying so. But I could never get them both down to the office together to sign the forms." Happy with Mimi, Lennon's nascent artistic abilities flowered: "I was passionate about *Alice In Wonderland* and drew all the characters," he recalled. "I did poems in the style of the Jabberwocky. I used to live *Alice*, and *Just William*. I wrote my own William stories, with me doing all the things."

But artiness didn't mean he was a shy, retiring boy; on the contrary, Lennon was soon getting into trouble: "The sort of gang I led went in for shoplifting and pulling girls' knickers down," he said. He was undeniably bright and had learned to read by the time he was four, consuming all the *Just William* serial adventures by Richmal Crompton, which detailed the domestic carnage of a naughty 11-year-old schoolboy. Lennon's boundless imagination took him a million miles away from the drab post-war suburbs of Liverpool. He even wrote his own books and

> **"Ugh, Beatles, how did the name arrive?… It came in a vision—a man appeared on a flaming pie and said unto them: 'From this day on you are Beatles'."**
> *Lennon on the birth of the band, writing for Mersey Beat magazine.*

comics, which Mimi still treasured years later. One was called *Sport & Speed Illustrated*, and at the end of one story was the caption: "If you liked this, come again next week. It'll be even better."

Lennon, however, didn't get better: when he

graduated from Dovedale Primary to nearby Quarry Bank High School he grew to be even naughtier than his fictional hero, William.

THE QUARRYMEN

"When I was about 12 I used to think I must be a genius, but nobody's noticed," said Lennon. "If there is such a thing as a genius, I am one, and if there isn't I don't care." It was an attitude that led him and his friends, Pete Shotton and Ivan Vaughan, to become the rebels of Quarry Bank, never more than one step away from a caning. His school reports grew steadily worse as he lived more and more in his dream world. When uncle George, who had always spoiled him with secret gifts of sweets and money, died in 1953, Lennon began to look towards his real mother for support.

Freddy Lennon had once taught his wife how to play the banjo, and Julia now passed on this knowledge to her son. Mimi and Julia have both been credited with buying him his first guitar—£10 (then US$40) from a mail order company, "guaranteed not to scratch". Mimi was always a strict disciplinarian—it was she who told Lennon that he would never make a living by playing the guitar—but carefree and reckless Julia helped to mould him into an outsider, although as many at the time testified, one with his own dangerous charm.

It seems odd that an outsider should be sociable enough to form a band, but rebellious schoolboys are often the nucleus of musical groups—and wanting to play rock music (or "beat music" as it was more commonly called) in the late-Fifties was like wearing your rebelliousness on your sleeve for the world to see. In 1955 Lennon got his first group together, the Quarrymen, the name inspired by their school, with his pal Pete Shotton on washboard.

The washboard—still then in practical use for scrubbing clothes clean in many poorer quarters of the UK—was an essential ingredient of the "skiffle" sound. Skiffle was a home-grown, rough-sounding descendant of Fifties US rock'n'roll—a cross between R&B and country—usually played on a cheap acoustic folk guitar, washboard and home-made, one-string, tea-chest bass—often all that was available to teenagers at the time. Skiffle, usually associated with the north of England, did make it to the south, eventually inspiring the sound of singers like Tommy Steele and Cliff Richard before records started arriving in larger quantities from the US to give them a taste of Buddy Holly and

The Quarrymen play a Liverpool gig on June 15, 1955. The line-up (L–R) was Eric Griffiths, Colin Hanton, Rod Davis, John Lennon, Pete Shotton and Len Garry. Shotton is playing washboard (just visible above Lennon's shoulder) and Gary a typical skiffle tea-chest bass.

Elvis Presley, but as a genre it is best exemplified by the songs of Lonnie Donegan.

Throughout his teenage years John always felt that he was different from the other kids—somehow he thought destiny had bigger things in store for him, and his skiffle music was the beginning of an outlet for his creativity. And he was right: despite failing all of his school exams—even art,

which was the only subject he really enjoyed—his new headmaster saw a glimmer of promise in him somewhere, and arranged for him to go to the local art college.

JOHN MEETS PAUL

As a young man, Paul McCartney's Irish father, Jim, was a cotton salesman working at Hannay's of Chapel Street in Liverpool by day, and a pianist leading the Jim Mac Jazz Band by night. Although he was credited as being hard working and responsible, he never settled down until he met Mary Mohin, a district health visitor. She was in her early thirties and he was almost 40 when they married in 1941. Their first son, James Paul, was born on June 18, 1942. The war had caused the Liverpool Cotton Exchange to close down, but Paul and his brother Michael (born two years later) never realized how hard their parents struggled to make a living.

Paul was quietly successful at primary school and went on to the city's largest college, the Liverpool Institute. In 1955, the McCartneys moved up in the world, to 20 Forthlin Road in Allerton, one of the city's more respectable suburbs. It seemed that the family's future was getting brighter—and then tragedy struck.

A lump in Mary's breast was diagnosed as cancer, and exploratory surgery proved useless. A month after feeling the first pains in her chest, Mary died, aged only 45.

McCartney's first guitar: although usually right-handed, he soon discovered he was a left-handed guitarist.

After his mother's death, McCartney escaped into a world of music, listening to Elvis and the Everly Brothers and teaching himself to play the guitar. "The minute he got the guitar, that was the end," said his brother. "He was lost. He didn't have time to eat or think about anything else. He played it on the lavatory, in the bath, everywhere."

In the summer of 1957, Ivan Vaughan introduced McCartney to John Lennon after a Quarrymen gig at a parish church fête. The two teenagers coolly acknowledged each other. Paul thought the band were pretty good, although their music was primitive—John played guitar like it was a banjo, with the sixth string just hanging loose. That afternoon, Paul showed him how to tune a guitar, and performed his party piece—a renowned impression of Little Richard. Paul felt that he had already matured beyond skiffle, but John was drinking beer after the performance and seemed very grown-up. A week later, Pete Shotton met Paul in the street and told him that he could join the band.

JOHN, PAUL AND GEORGE

As the Fifties drew to a close, the American music industry was trying desperately to tame rock'n'roll into a wholesome, marketable product

> **"He actually knew how to tune a guitar"**
> *Pete Shotton of The Quarrymen on meeting Paul McCartney*

with pretty, crooning young boys the nation's parents would welcome into their homes. In Britain, the record-buying teens flocked to see the UK's own boy-next-door, Cliff Richard.

Meanwhile, in Liverpool, R&B was still alive and well. The Quarrymen had a ready audience, if not always an enthusiastic one. McCartney's first uneventful appearance with the band was on October 18, 1957. As the two became friends, Lennon discovered McCartney's budding talent as a songwriter. Not to be bettered by this presumptuous youngster, he started to write words and melodies of his own. Soon they were spending all their spare time together and the relationship intensified after July 1958, when Lennon's mother was run down by an off-duty policeman and killed.

Other friends drifted out of his life. Only McCartney and a square, pale-skinned girlfriend called Cynthia Powell could see through his brash

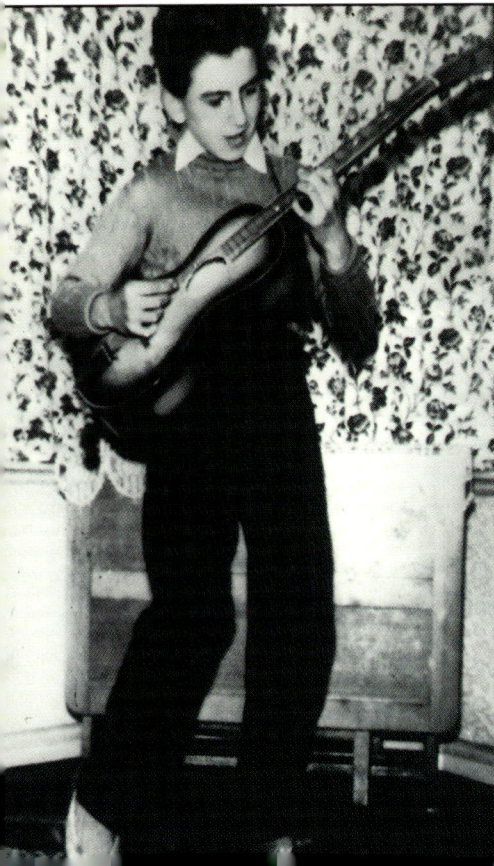

George Harrison, 12, plays his first guitar.

attitude. "My days with the group came to an end," said Pete Shotton, remembering his last, ragged Quarrymen performance at a local party. "John and I got hilarious, laughing like mad at each other's jokes. Then he broke my washboard over my head. I lay there, in tears, with it framed round my neck."

The core Quarrymen line-up now featured Lennon and McCartney on rhythm guitar and George Harrison on lead guitar. Harrison was a younger friend of McCartney's who had been hanging around with the band for months. When he joined in August 1958 he was only 15, and the supercilious Lennon took little interest in someone he thought of as a baby, a minnow.

The Harrisons were not very well off; Harrison senior drove one of Liverpool Corporation's green double-decker buses and his son earned pocket money as a butcher's errand boy in his spare time. George also had a particularly heavy version of the local Liverpudlian accent, known as Scouse, and insisted on keeping his Edwardian-style, slicked-back "teddy-boy" haircut to match his long-pointed "winkle-picker" shoes and brightly-coloured shirts and glitzy waistcoats. Although musicianship didn't come to him as naturally as it did to McCartney, Harrison was dedicated, and had constantly dreamed of joining the Quarrymen. Eventually, with the bribe of using Harrison's house for rehearsals, Lennon accepted him into the group.

CAREER OPPORTUNITIES

Anxious to forget their college school origins the band dropped the name the Quarrymen in 1959 and appeared under a series of aliases including the Rainbows and Johnny & The Moondogs. Lennon continued at art college (moving into an untidy flat in Gambier Terrace with his art college friend Stuart "Stu" Sutcliffe), while Harrison left Quarry Bank with no qualifications to take up an apprenticeship as an electrician. Supposedly this was useful to the band because he was put in charge of their equipment, sometimes wiring the guitars precariously into the microphone system when they had no amplifiers. McCartney passed only one subject—art—in his examinations but stayed on to resit them the following year, when he passed four more subjects so that he could stay on at school for another two years.

> ## "After the Beatles came on the scene everyone started putting on a Liverpudlian accent."
> *John Lennon*

The band continued to play working men's clubs and halls around Merseyside, entering talent competitions in the hope of winning money to buy more gear. They dressed as teddy-boy cowboys in black-and-white cowboy shirts with white tassles and bootlace ties—still very much the skiffle look. Most of their time was spent writing songs—more than 50 in the first couple of years John and Paul spent together, although only one of these early efforts, 'Love Me Do', ever got recorded.

At college, Lennon and his bohemian flatmate, Stu Sutcliffe, persuaded a student committee to purchase a tape recorder and PA system, which the band hijacked for their own gigs. Later, when Stu won an art prize for £60 (then US$240), Lennon convinced him to spend the money on an electric bass. Stu couldn't play a

note, but joined the Quarrymen nonetheless. Many band members had come and gone, and now the core line-up was John Lennon, Paul McCartney and George Harrison on guitar with Stu Sutcliffe on bass. They couldn't find a steady drummer, let alone a talented one, but they never seemed to care.

BIRTH OF THE BEETLES

With their engagements steadily increasing, the band still needed a recognizable name that broke them away from the locally well-known Quarry Bank High School. With more musical influences coming into Liverpool from across the Atlantic than from the UK itself, it wasn't surprising that US group names should have more impact on the boys. Lennon had always preferred the music of Buddy Holly to that of Elvis Presley, and it was he who came up with the variation on Holly's backing group, the Crickets. "The idea of beetles came into my head," said Lennon. "I decided to spell it BEAtles to make it look like beat music, just as a joke."

Stu Sutcliffe couldn't play a note, but Lennon persuaded him to join the Quarrymen as bass player.

The corny pun was not very popular outside the band to begin with, so they called themselves The Silver Beetles at their next important audition, an exclusive Liverpool performance for famous London promoter Larry Parnes, whose successful stable of UK crooners included the vividly named Tommy Steele, Billy Fury and Marty Wilde. The gig took place at the Blue Angel Club, owned by local entrepreneur Allan Williams, where four other groups were competing to support Billy Fury on a forthcoming national tour. In fact, Parnes didn't consider any of the bands were up to the job, but the Silver Beetles were offered a tour of Scotland backing his latest discovery, Johnny Gentle.

To be able to go on tour Harrison took two weeks off from his job, and McCartney somehow convinced his father that the school had given him a fortnight off to wind down before his exams. A stand-in drummer, Tommy Moore, came on tour with them—although the Silver Beetles proved to be unlucky for him. For a start at 36 he felt like an elderly bystander, and the rest of the band hardly knew him. When the reckless driving of Johnny Gentle caused the tour van to rear-end another vehicle, Moore's drum kit collapsed on him and knocked out his front teeth. After the tour he gave

Around Liverpool, Pete Best was always considered the best-looking and most popular Beatle.

Amid the seedy low-life of Hamburg's Reeperbahn, the five Beatles learned their trade: Pete Best, George Harrison, John Lennon, Paul McCartney and Stu Sutcliffe.

up rock'n'roll and returned to his job driving a fork-lift truck at a bottling works.

Unfortunately, the tour was a non-event for all involved. The others gave in to Lennon by slightly renaming themselves the Silver Beatles, and returned to the daily grind of playing working men's clubs around town.

THE FIFTH BEATLE

Mona Best owned a 14-room house in Hayman's Green in Liverpool's West Derby district. The place was so enormous that she decided to turn the basement into a coffee bar for teenagers, and it became the Casbah Club. The Quarrymen had hung out there, even lending a hand with the decoration, slapping paint around the cellar walls with help from Lennon's mousey girlfriend, Cynthia Powell.

Mona Best's son, Peter, was to become the drummer that the Silver Beatles had not realized they needed. The entrepreneur Allan Williams had been booking the band at his own coffee

> **"When I walk round I often think, "what's a scruff like me doing with this lot?" It soon passes. You get used to it."**
> *Ringo Starr*

house, The Jacaranda (where the basement murals had been painted by Lennon's flatmate Sutcliffe), and in August 1960 he offered them the chance to play live in Hamburg, West Germany. But he wanted a five-piece band. Suddenly, Pete Best and his shiny new drum kit were in.

Because of their merchant navy traditions, Liverpool and Hamburg had long been rival ports, and a Liverpool Scene was developing in Hamburg's low-life nightclubs. Twice the size of Liverpool, Hamburg had a notoriously seedy street life. The Reeperbahn was filled with bars and strip clubs, populated by gangsters, black-marketeers and illegal immigrants.

Dropping "The Silver" prefix, the Beatles started playing at a tiny club called the Indra, with their sleeping quarters in a shabby cinema, the

Richard Starkey onstage with Rory Storm & The Hurricanes: another Merseyside export

Bambi Kino, across the street, where they awoke each morning to the sound of Western B-movies and skin flicks. However, the long working day—playing eight-hour shows—gave them time to experiment and hone their craft as performers. As they learned to "Mach Schau" (make a show)—leap crazily around the stage like the other top local bands—their growing reputation around the city began to draw a crowd.

THE FOUR GET TOGETHER

The frenetic jumping up and down on stage—which later became a trademark of early Beatles fame—provided more than an entertainment, it also helped to keep steady their erratic timing when playing. On one occasion, it was also instrumental in causing a stage to collapse.

"The Germans really loved the Ray Charles classic 'What'd I Say'," said Pete Best, "because they could participate by echoing the lyrics and banging their beer bottles on the tables." If the bottles were in time, so were the Beatles. When the Indra closed down two months later after numerous complaints from local inhabitants about the noise, their promoter, Bruno Koschmider, moved them on to a larger club called the Kaiserkeller.

"I drank a lot," said Best. "You couldn't help it. They'd be sending us drinks up all the time, so we naturally drank too much. We had a lot of girls. We soon realized they were easy to get. Girls are girls, fellers are fellers. Everything improved a hundred percent. We'd been meek and mild musicians at first; now we became a powerhouse."

Along with other Liverpool bands like their friends Rory Storm & The Hurricanes, the Beatles developed a thriving, carefree rock'n'roll scene. When in October 1960 the bassist/vocalist from the Hurricanes, Lou Walters, nicknamed Wally, cut an amateur record with Lennon, McCartney and Harrison, he brought along his drummer, Richie Starkey—whose nickname was Ringo because of all the finger rings he wore. The recording was no grand affair—it was cut in a tiny recording booth behind Hamburg's main railway station—but it was the first ever recording by the fab four Beatles. Sadly, only one copy of the disc is known to have survived.

At the Kaiserkeller their work became harder still, with them often playing for up to 12 hours a night. "Your voice began to hurt with the pain of singing," said Lennon, later noted for his "leather lungs". The Beatles began experimenting with drugs—not for recreation, just to keep awake and

The first ever Beatle haircut, as worn by Stu Sutcliffe, was designed by his fiancée, the photographer Astrid Kirchherr (left). She pursued Stu shamelessly from the first moment of seeing him onstage in Hamburg.

alert. The local bands all used diet pills, amphetamines called Preludin, known as "Prellys", to stimulate them through the long working night. The young band—Sutcliffe as the eldest was only 20—were soon hardened by their experiences in Hamburg, surrounded as they were by free sex and overindulgence. The city was a breeding ground for talent, and the Beatles became one of its stars.

BACK TO THE MERSEY

Their raucous sound and behaviour both on and off the stage made them the darlings of Hamburg's cool avant garde art school set, which included Klaus Voorman and his girlfriend Astrid Kirchherr. Voorman, fascinated by rock music and the Beatles' leather-clad style, brought Astrid to the Kaiserkeller to see the band, and lost her there forever. "I fell in love with Stuart that very first night," she said. "He was so tiny but perfect, every feature." Astrid was an artist and photographer who had a creative vision of the band far beyond their good-time rock'n'roll.

She pursued Sutcliffe unashamedly and his was to be the first famous Beatle haircut and Beatle outfit— designed by Astrid. In November 1960, two months after their first meeting, the two became engaged. Sutcliffe had always been teased by the other Beatles. A genuine fine-art painter with a style all his own, he wasn't quite like the other Liverpudlians. He'd never pretended to be much of a musician, either, and despite playing hundreds of gigs his skills had scarcely improved—and now with his attachment to Astrid, Sutcliffe was even more the outsider, and McCartney began making it all too clear that he wanted to take over as the band's bassist.

When another local promoter convinced the band to end their stint with Bruno Koschmider at the Kaiserkeller and start playing at the Top Ten Club, Koschmider discovered that Harrison was only 17-years-old—too young to be in a German club after midnight. He was ordered to leave West Germany. A few days later, when Sutcliffe and McCartney returned to the Bambi Kino to collect their belongings, Koschmider had them arrested and deported.

IT'S MERSEY BEAT

On the Beatles' return to Liverpool, there was a sense of change in the air, not so much in the anodyne national music scene—which had hardly altered at all—but there was a feeling that the Merseyside beat groups had achieved a local character of their own and a critical mass that meant the "sound" was solidly different to anyone else's in Britain.

There was a new local weekly music paper called *Mersey Beat* to mark it. Whether the phrase "Mersey Beat" had grown up to become local parlance and given the paper its name, or whether it was the other way around, is debatable. But luckily for the prodigal Beatles its editor was an old flatmate of Lennon's from his Gambier Terrace days, and he used his influence to publicize the band. Indeed, the very first issue featured an article by John Lennon: *Being A Short Diversion On The Dubious Origins Of Beatles*.

Journeyman bands of the time hadn't reached a status much above that of suppliers of beat dance music, but at their first gig at Litherland Town Hall in Liverpool on December 27, 1960, the Beatles were billed as "Direct From Hamburg". It was a turning point. Promoter Brian Kelly couldn't believe his eyes as he watched dozens of screaming girls stop dancing and press themselves against the stage to be close to the band, the dance forgotten. Kelly booked the

Onstage in Hamburg in 1960, Lennon (still with "teddy boy" haircut), McCartney and Harrison try to keep time.

Beatles for 36 more dances over three months and established them as the premier rock band in the Merseyside area.

THE BEST OF CELLARS

The least likely of Liverpool venues was to become the Beatles' home from home, and their association with it would make it the most famous club in Britain, and later, throughout the rage of Beatlemania, the most famous club in the world.

It was The Cavern, on Mathew Street, and it was unlikely because for one it was tiny, and the Beatles were becoming big crowd pullers, and for

An early publicity shot, with Pete Best, sets the mood for the new Beatles' image.

not having broken in the UK at all (although it would later become a UK Number 1 hit for Brian Poole & The Tremeloes).

Although the group's families remained largely unimpressed, Mrs Harrison regularly stood in the crowd, screaming along with the local girls as sweat from the packed audience condensed on the low-arched ceilings and poured in streams down the cellar walls.

The Beatles first appearances at The Cavern ensured a regular tenancy, apart from a break through April, May and June, when they were once again offered a chance to play The Top Ten Club in Hamburg. This was a deal Sutcliffe had pressed for. He had been unable to return to art college in Liverpool, and with that disappointment added to his increasing dissatisfaction with being in the band, he could think only of returning to Hamburg to be with his fiancée, Astrid. The trip was to be marked by the Beatles' first ever professional recording.

They worked harder than ever, taking the stage at 7:00pm and alternating all night with

another it was known only for its full calendar of nationally acclaimed jazz bands. "We were always anti-jazz," said Lennon. "I think it's shit music, even more stupid than rock'n'roll, followed by students in Marks & Spencer [mass production stores] pullovers."

Their first date at The Cavern as the Beatles— they'd skiffled there as the Quarrymen three years earlier—was in February 1961, and new customers poured in from their very first performance. The set was as varied and wild as the Hamburg gigs, combining Lennon-McCartney songs and quirkily-arranged show tunes with US Top 20 hits like Chan Romero's 'Hippy Hippy Shake'. This was a particular McCartney favourite, all the better for

another British band, led by vocalist Tony Sheridan, until 3:00am. This time they slept in the club's attic—not exactly the Hilton, but a lot better than the Bambi Kino.

In Hamburg Sutcliffe led something of a double life, studying art by day and playing by night, almost without sleep. Gradually, he appeared onstage only infrequently, and eventually Paul McCartney got his way and took over the bass.

AIN'T SHE SWEET

Lennon and McCartney had written more than a hundred songs together since their first meeting, but they'd never made a professional recording until their return to Hamburg. It was a messy version of 'My Bonnie Lies Over The Ocean', featuring vocals by Tony Sheridan, who had been one of the big stars of the Hamburg scene from the beginning.

The West German bandleader Bert Kaempfert, who had recently scored a US Number 1 hit with 'Wonderland By Night', hired the Beatles to provide backing for the song, renaming them the

Tony Sheridan, then mistakenly credited for forming the original Beatles, sang the vocals for 'My Bonnie (Lies Over The Ocean)'.

Beat Brothers in the process. Despite the music's trite awfulness, they were thrilled to be recording. The businesslike bandleader even let them record in their own right—they played their old Quarrymen standby, 'Ain't She Sweet', and a throwaway Lennon-Harrison instrumental called 'Cry For A Shadow'.

Kaempfert was pleased enough with the results to invite them to record with him again and his eight Beatles recordings for Polydor Records inevitably reappeared in several different packages later when the band rocketed to

> ## "They had a rather untidy stage presentation…"
> *Brian Epstein, on first seeing the Beatles at The Cavern*

fame. A single of 'Ain't She Sweet' made it to Number 29 in the 1964 UK charts as something of a novelty record, much to Lennon's annoyance, who felt that it was no longer representative of the Beatles. He needn't have worried, ever-

Beatles manager to be: Brian Epstein's disinterest in rock music vanished forever when he first saw the Beatles play at a Cavern club lunchtime session

"They were scruffily dressed... but they had star quality," said Epstein. His promise was to make them famous.

eager fans were thrilled with it and in love enough with the Beatles to lap it up with the rest of Beatle-related collectables.

The Kaempfert recordings didn't mean much at the time, but they changed the Beatles' lives. 'My Bonnie...' even made it to the German Top 10. When the band returned to the UK in June 1961, Stuart Sutcliffe did not come with them—he stayed behind to marry Astrid and study art.

EPSTEIN STEPS IN

There are many ingredients that go into making a band truly successful: the energy and talent of the performers is obviously prime, but groups need musical and personal management to really bring out the best in them. The Beatles were

lucky in both these respects, first in their manager, Brian Epstein, then in their musical producer, George Martin.

According to his autobiography, Brian Epstein, the 27-year-old manager of NEMS (North End Music Stores), made his first visit to The Cavern on November 9, 1961 because he was curious about a band unknown to him who had been the subject of several enquiries in his record shop. Epstein was a regular contributor to *Mersey Beat*, but until that date had shown little or no interest in rock'n'roll music. On that November day, his first sight of the Beatles changed his mind.

"They were rather scruffily dressed," recalled Epstein, "in the nicest possible way, or, I should say, in the most attractive way: black leather jackets and jeans, long hair of course. And they had a rather untidy stage presentation... they had what I thought was a sort of presence and—this is a terribly vague term—star quality. Whatever that is, they had it, or I sensed that they had it."

Epstein tidied up the Beatles' sets and clothes, opting for the Kirchherr-styled mop-top haircuts, in time for the Mersey Beat poll winner's award, presented here in January 1962 by editor Bill Harry.

Epstein fought his way through to talk to what he took as the leader, Lennon, and despite his lack of experience, he promised the band increased performance fees and told them that he would use his influence as one of the North-West's biggest record retailers to get them a major British recording deal. In effect, he told the Beatles that he could make them famous. Their reaction was typical: politeness from McCartney, irreverence from Lennon and a mix of sceptical amusement from the rest—but they decided to let him have a go.

Lennon's cynical attitude was somewhat abashed as Epstein—seeming true to his word—secured the band their first major record label audition through a friend at Decca Records A&R on New Year's Day 1962. Their newly acquired road manager, Neil Aspinall, drove the band to London in his van, getting lost halfway in heavy snow, and eventually arriving at the Decca studio at 11:00am. In the hour-long session they recorded 15 songs chosen by Epstein to demonstrate their versatility, and included rock'n'roll, C&W,

It's hard to imagine what the upper-middle-class Epstein saw in this ragged rock band. At a typical Cavern gig the Beatles would drink, eat, smoke and sometimes even turn their backs on the audience to play for themselves—or for the girls they wanted to take home. Despite his shyness,

chart hits, and three Lennon-McCartney compositions: 'Hello Little Girl', 'Like Dreamers Do', and 'Love Of The Loved'. Their session was followed by an audition for Brian Poole & The Tremeloes, a band from the London suburb of Barking, and the Beatles were hustled out of the studio and back to Liverpool.

THE MAN WHO SAID, "YES"

On January 4, 1962 *Mersey Beat* published its first ever popularity poll, and the Beatles were clear winners. The next day, following Epstein's persuasion, Polydor (UK) released 'My Bonnie Lies Over The Ocean'—credited for the first time to Tony Sheridan & the Beatles.

At the NEMS office, after a Cavern lunchtime session on 24 January, 1962, the Beatles signed up with Epstein's new management company, NEMS Enterprises. From the very beginning, he insisted on cleaning up their act. He wanted them to change their onstage attitude, be smarter, more punctual, and keep to a strict set list, playing for no more than 60 minutes at a time. But in February came the bad news that Decca had rejected the Beatles in favour of The Tremeloes. It was Epstein's first failure as a band manager, and in response he angrily told the record company

that the Beatles were going to be "bigger than Elvis". Flushed and indignant, he bounced back by arranging an introduction to the head of A&R at Parlophone Records—the other man who was to become a major influence on their growth as artists—George Martin.

Martin was a career man with EMI's second-string specialist label, Parlophone. He knew little about pop music—his most successful records to date had been easy-listening and spoken-word comedy albums by Peter Sellers and Peter Ustinov—but when Brian Epstein played him the Beatles' Decca tapes, Martin heard something promising. When he met the boys themselves in June 1962, he found them instantly "charming". He had drawn up a recording contract on the strength of the Decca tapes alone, and after the boys played their first session at the Abbey Road studios in St Johns Wood, London, they thought they had a record deal.

George Martin thought otherwise. He was not impressed by Pete Best's erratic drumming and he was not entirely happy with their choice of material. But still, they seemed to have something.

Between their January date with Decca and meeting George Martin, the Beatles remained busy. Most significant of the concerts during spring was a performance at the Playhouse Theatre, Manchester, in March. First, the Beatles wore their matching £40 (then $US 160) grey, tweed suits with pencil-thin lapels and matching ties in public for the first time. Second, it was their debut recording for BBC Radio, the first of dozens of appearances—including their own series—in which they would perform many songs that were never officially released.

Then in April they flew from Manchester for another six-week enga-

gement in Hamburg to be greeted with tragic news from Astrid Kirchherr—Stuart Sutcliffe had died from a brain haemorrhage on April 10, 1962. He'd been plagued by increasingly painful headaches after suffering head injuries two years previously when he was attacked in a car park after a gig in Liverpool. He was just 21-years-old.

NOW WE ARE FOUR

Epstein was booking the Beatles for more engagements than ever before. Their first tour of ballrooms in the Top Rank chain (an offshoot of Rank, the British film-making and distribution company) began in June, taking them right across the UK. In eight weeks they performed 62 gigs as well as making their second recording session for BBC Radio. Their Cavern

> **"Even if Stuart had lived, he would have been blind and probably paralysed. He wouldn't have been able to paint. He would have preferred to die."**
> *Astrid Kirchherr*

Stu Sutcliffe's legacy is an art collection which has been exhibited worldwide.

New clothes from Austin Reed's, London, 1962. "For the first time in our lives, we could actually do something and earn money"—Paul McCartney

concerts were attracting such fanatical attendances that queues formed in Mathew Street hours before the Beatles took the stage. The venue had never been so popular.

Pete Best was the most publicly liked member of the band in Liverpool, but he had never shared the temperament and abilities of the others; while he had remained an amateur musician, they had become professionals; he was shy and retiring, they were loud and exuberant. He even refused to change his hairstyle to a Beatle cut. In the end, the rest of the band made a clean and ruthless break. Although Best had once acted as their manager,

drum kit at a gig in Birkenhead, near Liverpool.

The following week, a British crew from the Manchester-based independent television network company, Granada, filmed the Beatles playing at The Cavern. But once again the band missed their shot at TV exposure—lighting conditions in the cramped venue were considered so poor that the film couldn't be used, and it didn't resurface until the Beatles were famous when its flat, grainy quality mattered less than its rarity. On August 23, with Paul McCartney as best man, John Lennon married Cynthia Powell at the Mount Pleasant register office, where his mother had married his father 24 years before. He spent his honeymoon playing every night with the Beatles.

On September 4, 1962 the Beatles returned to London for their first proper Parlophone session. They recorded a song called 'How Do You Do It?', which George Martin thought could be a big hit for them, but put far more effort into their own song, 'Love Me Do'. Martin was still unhappy with the Beatles, and brought them back to Abbey Road a week later to try again, this time with a

had welcomed them into his own home—the Casbah—and played with them more than 200 times at The Cavern alone, Brian Epstein was given the unenviable task of sacking him on August 16, 1962.

Two days later, their old friend Richie "Ringo" Starkey, drummer from Rory Storm & The Hurricanes, took Best's place behind the

session drummer called Andy White, ousting Ringo from the drum stool to play tambourine. Perhaps because of his lack of beat music knowledge, Martin allowed the band to concentrate on perfecting 'Love Me Do'. It was to be a fateful decision, because the repetitive, upbeat number

with—for the time—unusual use of vocal harmonies and dominated by Lennon's rasping harmonica, was to blow pop music wide open.

LOVE ME DO

On Friday October 5 'Love Me Do' b/w 'PS I Love You' became the Beatles' first single, reaching Number 49 in the UK charts a week later and slowly climbing to reach Number 17 in

> **The Beatle jackets and haircuts were soon to become a famous sight worldwide.**

continue almost unbroken for more than three years. John Lennon spent his birthday—he was 22—with the band in London, talking to music journalists and recording for Radio Luxembourg. In Liverpool they appeared twice on the local TV show *People And Places* and continued to play all around the north of England, with only a two-week break at the Star Club in Hamburg.

Only slightly more confident of the band's commercial strength, Martin got the Beatles straight-back into the studio to record a follow-up, 'Please Please Me', and its B-side 'Ask Me Why'. Meanwhile the band continued to play every night until the end of the year. Just as 'Love Me Do' was reaching its peak in December, they set off for their fifth and final booking in Hamburg. The New Year's Eve gig at The Star Club was recorded by one of the other artists on the bill, and subsequently appeared as an unofficial live album.

According to many Beatleologists, Brian Epstein put the Beatles in the charts by ordering 10,000 copies of 'Love Me Do' for NEMS in

December. In retrospect, 'Love Me Do' hardly seemed to signal something unique—and its final chart position indicated that it failed to set all of Britain's teens alight—but to many at the time the combination of tunefulness, weird harmonies, the bluesy harmonica and Lennon's raspy-yet-yearning voice was a beacon in the dreariness of standard pop. Something amazing had happened, and it just remained to see whether these new Beatles could come up with more, or whether they were one-hit wonders.

They promptly began a series of engagements to promote the record, a publicity trail that would

Liverpool. If he did, the gamble certainly paid off in the long term. By 1963 he'd secured them a publishing deal, setting up a new company called Northern Songs.

Profits from the ownership of Lennon-McCartney music would be split with 50% to established music publisher Dick James, 20% each to Lennon and McCartney, and 10% to Epstein. For the era, it was a very generous deal, although none of the four partners could ever have imagined the value of their stake at the time. A first inkling came in early March 1963 when the second Beatles single, 'Please Please Me', went straight to Number 1 in the UK charts and the British press went Beatle-crazy.

When the Beatles appeared on *Thank Your Lucky Stars*, a popular British Saturday night TV show, in January 1963 it was their first major exposure in the UK media. Newspapers and radio were all very well, but nothing could compete with the power of television, and Britain had never seen anything like the Beatles before. Their hair was different, their suits were buttoned up to the neck, obscuring their ties, and their broad, playful grins captured the hearts of a nation's teenagers.

Within days, a semblance of what would become "Beatlemania" had started. TV show com-peres only had to say lines like: "…and now we've got four young musicians from Liverpool…" [faint screams of anticipation from the audience] "called John, Paul, George and Ringo…" [crescendo of screams, completely drowning out the compere's voice as he announces…] "the Beatles". From then on, the Fab Four would be simply known as "John, Paul, George and Ringo".

> **"Hello, this is John speaking with his voice. We're all very happy to be able to talk to you like this on this little bit of plastic..."**
> *from the first 'Beatles Christmas Record' (1963)*

The music press raved about them. In the London *Evening Standard*, Maureen Cleave described the band's looks as "beat-up and depraved in the nicest possible way". And so, in the midst of a flurry of excitement and triumph, they set off on their first real British tour supporting current British teen star, Helen Shapiro.

BEATLEMANIA

George Martin was encouraged by the Beatles' first UK Number 1 with 'Please Please Me', but he still wasn't confident. Anxious to make sure that it was not their last hit, he got them into the studio straight away to record their first album. However, instead of backing up 'Please Please Me' with a collection of hastily-recorded standards and show tunes, Martin was keen to recreate the atmosphere of the band's classic Cavern shows—he even considered recording the album at The Cavern itself.

In an era when singers, songwriters and musicians were usually three different sets of people, it was unprecedented to discover a British debut with so many original songs performed by the band. The entire album was recorded in one 13-hour session. Tracks like 'I Saw Her Standing There' came to them like a second language, played again and again on sweaty Hamburg nights.

Harrison got a chance at singing on 'Do You Want To Know A Secret?' and Ringo took a turn at the microphone with the stomping 'Boys'. The short 'Misery' was written on the

Recording numerous television shows would be the standard for early 1963.

tour for Helen Shapiro to sing but ended up as a close-harmony duet between John and Paul. The climax was the superb Isley Brothers' 'Twist And Shout'.

"John absolutely screamed it," said George Martin. "God knows what it did to his larynx, because it made a sound like tearing flesh. That had to be right on the first take." In fact John was suffering from a bad cold that day, which made his Hamburg-hardened singing voice all the more gravelly! The song became their early onstage

'Please Please Me' goes silver: with 250,000 sales, the Fab Four and George Martin receive their first silver platter to mark the occasion.

The four appear on BBC Television's *Juke Box Jury* **show on December 7, 1963.**

finale. *Please Please Me* was released on March 22, 1963 and became the best-selling UK album for 30 straight weeks until it was dislodged by its follow-up, *With the Beatles*.

EVERYTHING'S MERSEY

After recording *Please Please Me*, the Beatles went straight out on tour again. They were contracted to support headlining American acts Tommy Roe and Chris Montez, but inevitably the Beatles were given top billing. Roe and Montez went home at the end of March, leaving the Beatles to carry on without them. With support from Roy Orbison and fellow-Liverpudlians Gerry & The Pacemakers, they began their third tour of the year, taking in English ballrooms to the north, south, east and west.

Meanwhile, Brian Epstein was creating a stable of Merseyside artists which included Gerry Marsden, Cilla Black, Billy J Kramer & The Dakotas and the Fourmost, and he now had his own permanent office in London. Gerry & The Pacemakers released their first single, 'How Do You Do It?' (the song previously rejected by the Beatles) in 1963, and rocketed to Number 1 in the UK.

Immediately, the music press recognized a Liverpool scene. When the third Beatles single, 'From Me To You', also made Number 1 a month later, Gerry Marsden was still at Number 3 and the Mersey Sound had gripped Britain.

On radio and television, the Beatles charmed and upstaged everyone they met. They clowned around and ad-libbed wittily, and their glowing smiles won over every crowd. Meanwhile on August 3, at home in Liverpool, Cynthia Lennon gave birth to a son, Julian.

> **"We always got screams in Scotland. I suppose they haven't got much else to do up there."**
> *John Lennon*

The Beatles continued to play regularly at the Cavern Club until August 1963, but by then their popularity had outgrown it a hundred times over. Their fourth single, 'She Loves You', went to Number 1 in September and returned to the top spot a few weeks later (technically it was Number 1 even before its release based purely on advance orders). 'She Loves You' eventually sold more than 1.6 million copies, making it the best-selling single in the UK for the next 17 years.

Their appearance on British independent television network's *Sunday Night At The London Palladium* on October 13 was reported in every popular newspaper the next morning. According to the press, thousands of screaming teenagers—

They charmed the press, as the Beatlemania epidemic swept the UK.

mostly girls—had blocked the street outside the venue, desperate to catch the slightest glimpse of their idols. The success of 'She Loves You' changed the lives of the Fab Four forever. They would never again know the casual pleasure of walking down the street unaccosted, but at the time there was nothing more exciting happening in pop culture anywhere in the world. British newspaper the *Daily Mirror* coined the descriptive "Beatlemania" and gave name to an epidemic which swept the nation.

Towards the end of the year they headlined on the televized *Royal Variety Performance*, after which they were treated like royalty themselves. They charmed the press and television with their sly comments and witty one-liners. "The ones in the cheap seats clap their hands," implored John that night. "The rest of you, if you'd just rattle your jewellery." His gag was retold in every one of the morning papers, with the press loving the good-natured dig at the aristocracy from these Liverpool "scallywags", the salt of the earth. And their sharp wit didn't stop there.

"The French have not made up their minds

George answered critics by writing 'Don't Bother Me' for *With The Beatles.*

about the Beatles. What do you think of them?" asked one BBC interviewer. "Oh, we like the Beatles," John replied. "They're gear."

BRITAIN CONQUERED

On *Please Please Me*, the Beatles had rocked the system by making a long-playing (LP) record which was much more than a showcase for hit singles (Pop bands hadn't yet achieved the status

> **"An examination of the heart of the nation at this moment would find the name 'Beatles' upon it."**
> London Evening Standard, *Christmas 1963*

which allowed use of the more pretentious "album" to describe an LP. But with their second LP, they went a step further: *With The Beatles* didn't feature any British single releases at all. The seven new Lennon-McCartney tunes included the opening 'It Won't Be Long', with its trademark Beatles hook "Yeah (Yeah), Yeah (Yeah)"; 'I Wanna Be Your Man' sung by Ringo and sub-

Fooling around: the Beatles closed 1963 with their own musical pantomime in London.

sequently an important hit record for the Rolling Stones: and the fast-paced 'All My Loving', with George Harrison's country guitar break.

Silencing those fans who asked why he didn't write songs, George answered with 'Don't Bother Me', his first recorded Beatles song since 'Cry For A Shadow' with Bert Kaempfert. *With The Beatles* also included American rock'n'roll hits like 'Roll Over Beethoven' and 'You Really Got A Hold On Me'—old standards that were a throwback to 274 nights in Hamburg.

Beatlemania seemed good for everyone, with record sales going through the roof. But the constant attention began to wear the Fab Four very thin. Their success continued in November as *With The Beatles* went straight to Number 1 in the UK album chart. Their fifth single, 'I Want To Hold Your Hand', finally knocked 'She Loves You' from the Number 1 position in the UK following advance orders of almost a million copies.

By the end of 1963 they had accrued 2.5 million record sales from 'I Want To Hold Your Hand' and 'She Loves You' in the UK alone, holding the Number 1 spot on the single and album

charts for almost six months. The autumn was spent on a 32-date twice-nightly tour of British venues, followed by the *Beatles Christmas Show*, a festive, musical pantomime in London. They had unquestionably broken the British market.

The USA was next…

CAPITOL GAINS

America proved to be very unwelcoming at first. Parlophone's huge American sibling, Capitol Records, had so far been unmoved by the Beatles.

Waving to thousands of hysterical fans at New York's John F Kennedy airport

Wise-cracking with US TV show host Ed Sullivan, as 70 million American teenagers tuned in to watch the phenomenal new stars.

They declined to release 'Love Me Do' or 'Please Please Me' in the US and Brian Epstein had only managed to arrange for minor releases on the Vee Jay label, with no great success. However, when DJs began playing imported copies of 'I Want To Hold Your Hand' on radio stations all around the country, Capitol could hardly wait to get the Beatles across the Atlantic.

> ## "They've got everything over there. What do they want us for?"
> *George Harrison on US Beatlemania in 1964*

In an unprecedented flurry of activity, a million copies of the single were pressed and Capitol allocated $50,000 (over £500,000 by today's standards) for a massive *The Beatles Are Coming* publicity campaign. Meanwhile, a representative of the band's merchandizing company, Seltaeb ("Beatles" backwards), was licensing Beatles

Ed Sullivan gets the first US interview with America's new heroes.

Their arrival at John F Kennedy Airport in New York was yet another historical, hysterical landmark in Beatlemania history. On the (probably unnecessary) promise of a free T-shirt for every fan there to greet the band, the terminal was crammed with 3,000 screaming girls as well as reporters and determined photographers. Their appearance on *The Ed Sullivan Show* next day was watched by 70 million and the evening was marked by a recognizable decline in juvenile crime nationwide. The Beatles travelled to Washington DC for their first-ever US concert at products nationwide. The first million Beatles T-shirts had all been sold within three days of arriving in the stores. The epidemic was spreading.

By the time the group arrived in America on February 7, 1964, they were already Number 1 in the US singles chart, and their first two American albums, *Meet The Beatles!* and *Introducing...The Beatles*, both put together from British Beatle releases, were climbing steadily, reaching Number 1 and Number 2 respectively in March.

A widely-used shot of the time: the Beatles prepare for a snowball fight outside the Washington Coliseum, February 1964.

the 7,000-capacity Coliseum. It was just like being in Britain—only more so. The screaming was so loud that the audience could barely hear the music, which was probably just as well because even the band couldn't hear what they were playing.

THEY KNOW US ALL

A glut of records suddenly took the US charts by storm. On April 4, 1964, the Beatles held the top five places in the singles chart. A week later, 14 of the Top 100 singles were Beatles songs. America had never witnessed such an overnight success. The world had never seen anything like the Beatles. "We thought we'd have to grow on everybody," said John to one TV reporter, "but everybody seems to know us all. It's as if we'd been here for years—it's great."

When they returned to Britain as conquering heroes to another throng of screaming fans at Heathrow, they were hustled directly to the Abbey Road studios, and then to the set of their first movie, *A Hard Day's Night*. Amid all the bizarre showbiz glitter, John Lennon's first book, punningly titled *In His Own Write*, was published

Heroes' return: the Fab Four arrive at Liverpool's Speke airport, 11 August, 1964, from their triumphant US visit. It was the last time they would call Liverpool a "home" to return to.

in March and rose to the top of the best-seller list. It seemed there was nothing a Beatle could not do, but the first signs of stress were beginning to make themselves felt: just before the group set off for their first world tour, Ringo was taken ill with tonsilitis and missed most of the dates, rejoining the band only in Melbourne, Australia. It was a circus tour, surrounded by explosions of press fervour all round the world.

The Beatles' suits and Beatles' Cuban-heeled boots sold in their thousands, and while everyone was expecting it all to come to an end, it just went on and on. Years later, a cynical John Lennon recalled the time when the gravy train seemed to be unstoppable: "We were the Caesars," he said. "Who was going to knock us when there were millions of pounds to be made? All the handouts, the bribery, the police, all the fucking hype. Everybody wanted in."

SMILING FOR THE CAMERAS

The world tour schedule was gruelling, covering Scandinavia, Holland, the Far East and Australasia. In Adelaide a crowd estimated at 300,000 congregated outside their hotel. In Melbourne there were as many as 250,000. The Beatles were expected to grin and clown in front of the dignitaries of every city, comforting the disabled, kissing babies like a party of royal visitors and holding forth on the iniquities of the H-bomb. Despite the veil of glamour, many people were physically hurt in the crowds, not least the group themselves, who were groped and screamed at all around the world.

The movie *A Hard Day's Night*—named after a favourite phrase of Ringo's—showed mostly only the fun side of being a Beatle, reinforcing their good-natured image. Described by influential American film critic Andrew Sarris as "the *Citizen Kane* of jukebox musicals", it was directed by Dick (Richard) Lester in six weeks from a script by Liverpudlian screenwriter Alun Owen. The soundtrack featured the unforgettable title track (an instantly recognizable number, right from the clanging intro of the first chord) and 'Can't Buy Me Love', both Number 1 singles in the US and UK.

A Hard Day's Night is the story of a "typical day in the life" of a fictionalized Beatles (but

Treated like royalty: at the London movie premiere with Her Royal Highness Princess Margaret. "It's as good as anybody who can't act," said John.

and although the movie looks and sounds dated today, its surreal imagery still manages to evoke the claustrophobic sensation of being trapped in a situation not entirely of the Beatles' making—fun, yes, but the fun has a hard edge and it's not entirely comfortable.

shot in a documentary style, which convinced fans that this *was* the real thing), peppered with absurd slapstick and cheeky jokes: "How did you find America?" asks one pompous reporter in the movie. "Turn left at Greenland," replies John; "I fought the war for people like you," says a sour-faced old man. "Bet you're sorry you won," comes the reply. Dick Lester, slightly known at the time for his off-beat sense of comedy, meshed well with the feel of being a Beatle,

London's Piccadilly Circus is thronged by 200,000 fans on July 6, 1964 for the Royal premiere of *A Hard Day's Night.*

BeatLes!

BEATLES BEDLAM

A 22,000-mile, 23-city tour of North America followed in August 1964. In four months the Beatles had played on four continents in over 50 cities. The hysteria in the USA was more bizarre than ever. Fans in Dallas forced their way on to the airport runway so they could clamber onto the wings of the group's chartered Lockheed Elektra. Exclusive tour souvenirs included the Beatles' hotel bed-sheets, cut into hundreds of tiny squares and framed with an affidavit of authenticity. For one concert in Kansas City the group were paid $150,000 (over £1.5 million by today's standards) for a single appearance—the highest fee ever paid in America for one show.

John, Paul, George and Ringo were forced to resort to all kinds of deceits to fool over-eager fans about their movements. "There was one near escape at the Cow Palace [San Francisco]," said Ringo. "The crowds surged forward and got on the limousine we were supposed to be in.

Relaxation on the 1964 US tour in August only came in hotels or during sound-check breaks at auditoriums.

They squashed the roof in. We could have been killed, but we were safe in an ambulance with seven sailors. That's how they were smuggling us that time."

The touring continued back in the UK, ending the year with *Another Beatles Christmas Show* at

Classic early-Beatles television appearance

the Odeon, Hammersmith, London, twice-nightly for 20 nights. Their touring schedule had been gruelling, but Parlophone hurried them straight back into the studio to get a single and album out before Christmas. Indeed, this pattern lasted throughout the group's career and more than half of their albums were released in the last two months of each year.

The single, 'I Feel Fine', which appeared on none of their albums, topped the charts worldwide at the end of the year. Beginning with a whine of feedback from George's guitar which distorted sublimely into the song's melodic riff, 'I Feel Fine' was the most mature Beatles single to date.

The LP *Beatles For Sale*, however, showed glum faces on the cover—an indication, perhaps, that they were working too hard for their fame. 'Babies In Black' and the Dylan-influenced 'I'm A Loser' presented a pessimistic side of the band which 'I Wanna Hold Your Hand' and the chirpy hits of 1963 had kept hidden. In retrospect it's

Hotel room after hotel room: touring and recording were beginning to pall. Brian Epstein and the boys check out yet more publicity stills.

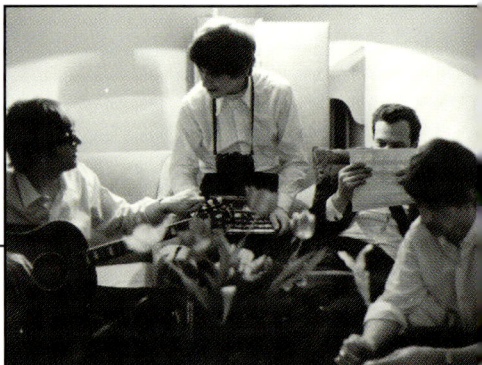

obvious that the sessions lacked the energy of their first three albums. And the title had a double-meaning you didn't need to look too closely to understand—the Beatles were enjoying the financial benefits of selling themselves, but they realized even then that there was only so much they could give.

BACK BEFORE THE CAMERAS

They weren't about to let up, and commenced shooting a second movie, aptly titled *Help!*, which would be released in mid-1965. To fit the group's progressive philosophy, their second film had to be different from the gritty quality of *A Hard Day's Night*. Directing again, with ten times the budget, Dick Lester opted for colour instead of black-and-white and leant more towards the now well established thrills'n'spills of a James Bond-style plot—albeit as a pastiche.

The boys get a quiet moment on an exotic location by the sea while shooting *Help!*.

> **"They were high all the time we were shooting. But there was no harm in it then. It was a happy high."**
> *Richard Lester, after directing* Help!

The screenplay lifted the Beatles from the familiar backdrop of grey British streets and dropped them into the exotic scenery of the Bahamas and Obertauern, a picturesque resort in the Austrian Alps. Where *A Hard Day's Night* had been a credible-looking mock-documentary, *Help!* was one, long, madcap chase involving a mad scientist, anarchistic terrorists and a selection of bad guys all determined to capture the magical ring on Ringo's finger. As Beatle biographer Philip Norman recalled, *Help!* was "Swinging London personified—part-music, part-colour sup-

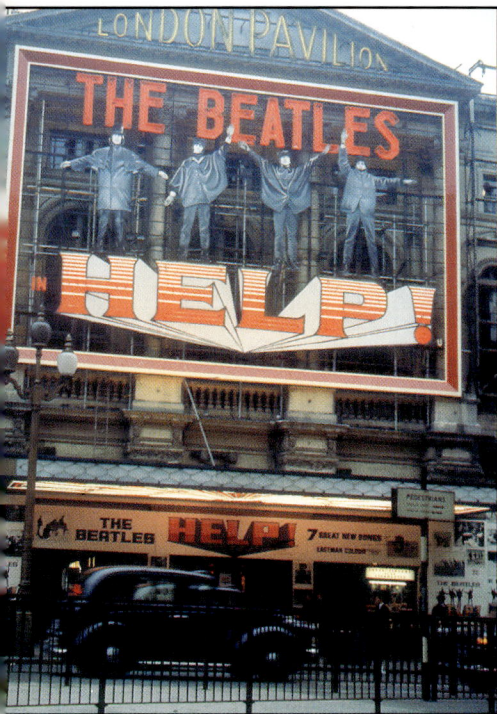

Help! **opens at the London Pavilion, Piccadilly Circus, July 29, 1965.**

plement travelogue, part-Pop Art strip cartoon".

The film gave fans seven new songs, joined on the *Help!* LP by seven more. John and Paul had rarely ever composed songs in each other's presence, but always competed against each other, two fertile minds nourishing one another, but on *Help!* Paul's song 'Yesterday' was different. It was "not a Beatles song" according to George

> ## "I'll keep it to dust when I'm old."
> *Ringo Starr on his MBE*

Martin. The first recording session took place with no other members of the group, featuring only a string quartet, with music arranged by Paul and George Martin. John's haunting 'You've Got To Hide Your Love Away' was a raw antidote to the delicate beauty of 'Yesterday', and indicative of Bob Dylan's influence on the Lennon style.

Although the LP featured tracks which recalled the days when playing together on a stage was all they lived for, like the Cavern classic 'Dizzy Miss Lizzy' and the relentless title track, the pleasure of performance was slipping away with every concert. Only within the comforting

Amid controversy, the Beatles received MBE medals in the Queen's 1965 birthday honours list.

walls of their studio could they escape the piercing screams of Beatles fans. Abbey Road was to become a haven in which their genius would begin to blossom.

BY APPOINTMENT TO HER MAJESTY

In June it was announced that the Beatles were to be awarded medals making each a Most Excellent Member Of The British Empire (MBE) in the Queen's 1965 birthday honours list. To much publicity—both good and bad (some war veterans threatened to return their medals)—they were pre-

A year after their first US tour, the Beatles were back, seen here during a sound check, to play vast arenas.

sented with their MBEs at Buckingham Palace in October, an event which only bemused them: "I thought you had to drive tanks and win wars to win the MBE," said John, only further exacerbating the anger of would-be medal returners. No doubt engineered by Labour Prime Minister Harold Wilson, the award was a recognition of, and tribute to, a new kind of British export.

A short European tour followed, notable only for failing to sell out (one matinee performance in

Drowned by non-stop screaming from 55,000 fans, musicianship seemed unnecessary at the record-breaking Shea Stadium concert on August 15, 1965.

fears about filling such a giant auditorium, they were quickly dispelled as the Beatles performed in front of 55,600 fans. The show opened with 'Twist And Shout' and 'She's A Woman', blasting into a wall of screams.

The concert was filmed by BBC Television using 12 cameras and transmitted as *The Beatles*

> ## "I've had caviar and I like it. But I'd still rather have an egg sandwich."
> *George Harrison in the* London Evening Standard

Live At Shea Stadium, capturing not only the blind hysteria of the huge audience safely penned in behind high metal fences—doing their desperate best to clamber over them—but also the phlegmatic indifference of the band. Graphic equalizers were then only in their infancy, but many disgruntled "serious" Beatles fans didn't need to phase out the deafening audience noise to insist that "you could clearly hear they weren't playing well".

Two weeks later the Beatles had worked their way to the USA's West Coast to play two

Genoa, Italy, attracted only 5,000 spectators to a 25,000-seat arena) but in August the group returned to the USA, where Beatlemania was raging as intensely as ever.

The tour began with a record-breaking performance at Shea Stadium in New York (home of the Mets baseball team). It was a new kind of venue for pop music groups, but if there were any

nights at the imposing Hollywood Bowl, from which live recordings resurfaced over a decade later on the *Beatles Live At The Hollywood Bowl* album in 1977.

YOU WON'T SEE ME

The group were contractually obliged to conjure up a new LP before Christmas, and with little new material in stock, they spent more than a month recording and writing new songs for what would become *Rubber Soul*. By the end of 1965, the Beatles had lost much of their collective energy, but each had discovered new forms of inspiration to spice up the long recording sessions.

John was freely experimenting with LSD, "acid" as it was commonly referred to, the mind-expanding hallucinogenic drug which was still legal in the UK. He'd also been writing again, and in July published a second book, this time a slim volume of nonsense-poetry with another punning title: *A Spaniard In The Works*. George had discovered the sitar while filming *Help!*, and its appearance on John's hollow 'Norwegian Wood'

Paul made time off to spend with his fashionable girlfriend, British actress Jane Asher.

finally allowed George to make a unique contribution to the Beatles. Paul increasingly spent his time with the privileged family of his girlfriend, actress Jane Asher, struggling to educate himself into the British upper class. Ringo, meanwhile, wanted only to enjoy the fruits of his labours, understanding little of the others' aspirations.

Rubber Soul was a quieter album, characterized by the introspection of George's 'If I Needed Someone' and John's 'Nowhere Man'. The realization soon hit them that such intricate, personal ballads as 'In My Life' could never be performed before an audience of wailing teenagers. Thus were sown the seeds for the

Beatles' retirement from the stage. At the end of 1965, there was a brief tour of Britain, playing only eight cities, with a set list of only 11 songs, mostly old favourites—which was fine, because that was all the crowd really wanted to hear.

No one but John, Paul, George and Ringo knew this was to be their final British tour. But despite their intention to quit the live circuit, the band still had commitments. Their first and only shows in Japan—five nights at the 10,000-capacity Nippon Budokan Hall—were patrolled by an astonishing force of 3,000 policemen, necessitating the most restrained exhibition of Beatlemania

ever seen. Perhaps a more low-key approach was overdue: in June 1966 the Beatle craze turned sour. On their visit to the Philippines they accidentally snubbed First Lady Imelda Marcos when they failed to appear at a reception at Malacanang Palace. They had to buy their way out of the country, and an angry crowd greeted them at the airport, where Brian Epstein and the Beatles' trusty bodyguard, Mal Evans, were beaten and kicked. Athough they didn't know it, the violence was about to spread to the United States.

THE NEW MESSIAHS?

In an interview with Maureen Cleave for the London *Evening Standard* John had been asked for his comments on the decline of western religion. "Christianity will go," he responded. "It will vanish and shrink. I needn't argue with that… We're more popular than Jesus now." It was a typical acidic Lennon commentary on the absurdity of pop culture and in Britain his words went largely unnoticed, but months later, in July

As they started sessions for 'Paperback Writer', recorded in two days, it was obvious that the studio had become more important to them than playing live.

John explains to the press just what went wrong on the Philippines visit.

misunderstanding; it merely strengthened the bars on their private prison cell. Their performances were short, rudimentary, lacklustre and seldom to a capacity crowd. Throughout the tour, they were in fear of a crazed sniper in the audience. So, on August 29, 1966, when the Beatles took the stage at Candlestick Park in San Francisco, it was for their final concert performance, lasting only 33 minutes. From this time on, the record buyers would become the real audience for Beatles music, and their own imaginations rather than the thrill of live performances the creative drive— away from the pressures of the public.

1966, the interview was misquoted by American teen magazine *Datebook*. The media's uproar against the band, and John in particular, was matched only by the excitement over the Beatles' return tour of the US in August. In Birmingham, Alabama, Beatles records were being ceremonially burned, and genuine threats of violence flooded in.

Brian Epstein was terrified that one of his boys would get hurt, and called a special press conference to try to explain John's comments. However, the Beatles' popularity was barely affected by this

> **"The record burning was a real shock. I couldn't bear knowing I created another little place of hate in the world."**
> *John Lennon on reactions to his Jesus Christ statement*

The individuals appear; gone are the mop-tops and jackets, and with 'Paperback Writer' topping UK and US charts, it's off on tour again—but for the last time.

monies and harsh, chugging guitar riff were unlike anything they had played before, linking them more to the force of rebellious British rock bands like the Rolling Stones and the Who.

TOMORROW NEVER KNOWS

Revolver was the brilliant result of the band's new-found freedom from touring. The LP sleeve was a psychedelic collage of line drawings, mostly cartoons, by their old Hamburg friend Klaus Voorman, with an outstanding conceit—so

The new Beatles sound had already been previewed with the spring USA and UK Number 1 hit, 'Paperback Writer'. It was unusual in that it was the first of their singles not to have a lovesong lyric, and its Beach Boys-style har-

> **Teenage girls had always loved Paul, but with his bitter-sweet ballad, 'Eleanor Rigby', even the mums queued for an autograph.**

famous were the Fab Four, so naturally awaited the album, that they only bothered to print the Beatles' name on the back cover.

Opening with George's 'Taxman', an unambiguous social comment, the album—it was seriously the first LP that deserved the epithet "album", as if it were a concentrated work of art—immediately changed pace with Paul's classic ballad 'Eleanor Rigby', which was issued as a single on the same day as the album, backed with 'Yellow Submarine' sung by Ringo. John's off-beat inspiration led to the drug-influenced 'She Said She Said' and the explosive closing track, 'Tomorrow Never Knows', with its backward-tracked guitar sounds, an inspiration for the coming psychedelic age.

For the Christmas market, a British album was released called *A Collection Of Beatles Oldies But Goldies*, which brought together the non-album tracks 'She Loves You', 'From Me To You', 'We

Can Work It Out', 'I Feel Fine', 'Bad Boy', 'Day Tripper', 'Paperback Writer' and 'I Want To Hold Your Hand'. It was a fitting end to an era which had changed pop music irrevocably; but there was no doubt that the era *did* have to end.

The first apparent change—fans were still expecting more tours to follow—came when John went off to Spain on his own to appear in Dick (now Richard) Lester's movie *How I Won The War*. It was a harsh black-comedy attack on war, in which John acted the part of Private Gripweed. For this role he had to cut his hair very short and wear wire-rimmed spectacles to compensate for his dreadful eyesight. When filming was com-

> **John and George collaborate on Revolver, the first LP to deserve the name "album".**

January 21, 1966: George marries Pattie Boyd in Surrey, England in a blaze of publicity. It was to be the start of a Beatles' break-up as they went their own ways—George to India.

In 1966 the Beatles quit live performances, drained by more than 1,400 appearances. This "new look" photo was an attempt to disprove rumours of a break-up.

plete, the hair and glasses remained. The mop-top was gone for good.

Next to go was George. Still only 23-years-old, and now married to Pattie Boyd, the bit-part actress turned fashion model he'd met while filming *A Hard Day's Night*. George set off for India in search of the gurus who *really* played the sitar. His pilgrimage required shrugging off the trappings and chains of superstardom to take a more humble role as student under the tuition of Ravi Shankar, and becoming immersed in yoga philosophy and disciplines. Ironically, his visit had a rebound effect, making Ravi Shankar a world-famous star who later took to touring in his own right.

Paul escaped the Beatles in his own way by living the life of a London gentleman in his high-walled, guarded St John's Wood town house, a stone's throw from the Abbey Road studios and writing the score for a new British film called *The Family Way*. Like the others, Paul grew a moustache, and began to dress in high-Sixties camp-military fashions from Swingin' London's Carnaby Street. Meanwhile, comfortable in his Surrey home, Ringo settled down with his wife Maureen and their baby son Zak.

ACID NOSTALGIA

After several months apart, the Beatles came together again and commenced a frenzy of recording, a process which now frequently went on all night. John's song 'Strawberry Fields' was

an acid-flavoured reminiscence about a boys' reformatory near Mimi's home in Woolton. From the complexities of *Revolver* songs, it seamlessly went up the scale, adding more fuel to the critical fire that the Beatles were not so much a pop band as a multi-cellular classic composer. But the song also had a touch of the musical megalomania that would culminate in *Sgt. Pepper's Lonely Hearts Club Band*. One of the most complicated of all Beatles songs to record, thanks to John's imagination and George Martin's skill in the studio 'Strawberry Fields' was hailed as a new pinnacle in recording achievement.

Paul's 'Penny Lane'—typically far less obscure than John's vision of the past (Paul was not yet experimenting with LSD)—was another piece of nostalgia. Penny Lane was a familiar place for all the Beatles and the song recreates the landscape of their ordinary, suburban Forties childhood. It was a normality from which they had yearned to escape, and to which they could never return, even if they wanted to.

Parlophone, desperate for new material, released 'Strawberry Fields' and 'Penny Lane' together as a single in February 1967. It reached Number 1 in the USA, but in the UK only managed Number 2, breaking the series of consecutive Number 1 hits which they had sustained since 'Please Please Me' way back in 1962.

Innovation in music wasn't the Beatles' only contribution to Sixties popular culture. To avoid an inevitable live appearance on BBC Television's *Top Of The Pops*, they had films made of both songs, though most notably of 'Strawberry Fields'. They can be seen mouthing the words and apparently playing instruments, but the outdoors, dreamscape images, dripping in surrealism, made the film far more than a mere substitute for their presence in the studio. In most respects this was one of the first ever promotional "videos", which later would become the staple of the pop industry.

LOOKING FOR A CONCEPT

Meanwhile, the recording sessions continued aimlessly, news which leaked to the music press, eager for another album. For months rumours were ripe of imminent launches, only to be dashed by official spokesmen claiming that the Beatles would release when they were ready and not before.

> ## "The bigger we got, the more unreality we had to face..."
> *John Lennon*

And the Beatles were not ready. Studio jam sessions gelled into songs, but none of the group felt that the collection had any coherence, and after *Revolver* a "concept"—some red thread to tie it all up—seemed paramount. First, a song which Paul had written in the Cavern days, 'When I'm Sixty-Four', made a humorous reappearence, a blast from the past. Totally unlike 'When I'm Sixty-Four' was 'A Day In The Life', a now rare collaboration between John and Paul, it was destined to become one of their most original and influential tracks. To the mixed bemusement of George and Ringo, Paul requested a 40-piece orchestra, and asked George Martin to conduct a 12-bar sequence in which each musician gradually built up from the quietest, lowest

A place to which they could never return: surrealism and nostalgia mixed dreamily in the 1967 promotional movies for 'Penny Lane' and 'Strawberry Fields Forever".

sound his instrument could make to the loudest, highest pitch. John said he wanted to hear a "musical orgasm".

The result was unlike anything that had ever been heard on a pop record before. But still there was no concept—until Paul came up with the jaunty-but-sad 'Sgt. Pepper's Lonely Hearts Club Band', which was to become the album's eponymous track. Its imagery and feel propelled the group into renewed excitement. What if the album were presented as though Sgt. Pepper had recorded it? They could try overdubbing sound effects and make it sound like a live concert. "From that moment," said George Martin, "it was as if Pepper had a life of its own."

That simple idea transformed *Sgt. Pepper's Lonely Hearts Club Band* into one of landmarks in the history of recording. The Beatles were not the first band to produce an album for the psychedelic generation. On the US West Coast, The Grateful Dead were at the centre of a rapidly growing international hippy culture, while bands like Big Brother & The Holding Company experi-

mented freely with lightshows at their gigs to try to recreate visually the effects of experiencing LSD. But the Beatles had more influence than any other pop group in history, and so it is *Sgt. Pepper's Lonely Hearts Club Band* which has endured as *the* time-capsule of the late-Sixties, capturing the style and aspirations of the age.

FIXING A HOLE

On May 26, 1967, millions of teenage fans came of age by listening to the sound of one glorious sliver of black vinyl. It was the first work of art from a type of music which had never been considered an art form before. *Sgt. Pepper...* blew away the record industry's cobwebs and has remained relevant for more than 25 years.

Hundreds of hours of playing—not in a studio but *with* a studio—had paid off. The Beatles

Ambassadors of psychedelic style, George and Ringo get ready for a summer of love.

had they had CD technology, not even the break to turn over the record would have happened. Even at the end they turned the run-off groove into an endless spiral of noise, simultaneously challenging expectations and playing a cheeky student trick.

Breaking with tradition, none of the songs were released as singles, or even as part of an EP (Extended Play) record. Even the extravagant gatefold sleeve was a revelation, featuring artwork by pop artist Peter Blake, which set the band within a living collage of Beatle iconography. The back cover featured the lyrics of the songs, a bold

experimented with the capabilities of stereo, shifting a sound from one speaker to another, as they had attempted with 'Good Day Sunshine' on *Revolver*, only to far greater and more emotional effect. They played clever games with sounds and effects to blend one track seamlessly into the next. It's fruitless but interesting to speculate that

Aping a live performance: to promote 'Hello, Goodbye', the Beatles made three film clips —here seen in Sgt. Pepper uniforms for the US release in November 1967.

statement of their originality. Most significantly of all, they proved that a pop album could concern itself with subjects other than love songs, and 'Lucy In The Sky With Diamonds' revealed John Lennon to be no less an artist than fellow surrealist Salvador Dali.

'Being For The Benefit Of Mr Kite' continued the album's bizarre circus theme, the words being taken from an old fairground poster John had on his wall, backed by a duet of two keyboards and cut-and-pasted steam organ sounds blended together into the chaotic hustle of a crowded big top.

No other record before or since has been greeted with such overwhelming critical approval. Reactionaries within the media, perhaps scared or overwhelmed by its potency, banned it from the radio. 'Lucy In The Sky With Diamonds' was an obvious target for a first assault (the initial letters L... S... D..., surely no coincidence, despite the band's strenous denials), but even Paul's seemingly innocuous 'Fixing A Hole' was read as an allegory of heroin injection.

However, BBC radio could not dilute the effects of this music so easily. As psychedelic guru Dr Timothy Leary pompously announced: "The Beatles are mutants. Prototypes of evolutionary agents sent by God with a mysterious power to create a new species—a young race of laughing freemen... They are the wisest, holiest, most effective avatars the human race has ever produced."

LOVE IS ALL YOU NEED

At the very peak of the Beatles' career, modern communications technology gave them the opportunity to spread the message of what would become known as "the summer of love" all around the globe. *Our World* was a worldwide satellite TV broadcast—the first ever—on Sunday June 25, 1967, for which the Beatles were chosen to represent the United Kingdom by singing their specially composed song 'All You Need Is Love'. Surrounded by their friends, the band performed to an audience of more than 200 million viewers (possibly as many as 400 million). They were supported by a 13-piece orchestra and their backing singers included Jane Asher, Mike McCartney, Pattie Harrison, Mick Jagger, Marianne Faithfull, Keith Richard, Graham Nash, Eric Clapton and Keith Moon. It was the highest point in the band's showbiz career... but it didn't last long.

In August, the Beatles met with considerable derision over their involvement with Indian guru Maharishi Mahesh Yogi, who invited the band to be indoctrinated in his teachings at a conference in Bangor, Wales. George, who had come across the Maharishi during his Indian visit, was largely responsible for the introductions, but John became an avid convert. At the time, in public, it also seemed that Paul and Ringo were pinning their hopes on the wisdom of this bizarre eastern prophet, but dissensions among the Beatles were already starting to show, and the Bangor trip was merely to exacerbate them.

However much some laughed at it all, it fitted perfectly with the new-age hippy cult, where Indian mandalas decorated many an apartment and Indian mantras and sitar music had become the order of the day. The Beatles were tuning in and dropping out, and the Maharishi's message made sense: "What he says about life and the universe is the same message that Jesus, Buddha

Indian guru, Maharishi Mahesh Yogi, indoctrinated the Beatles into transcendental meditation in August 1967 at Bangor, Wales.

and Krishna and all the big boys were putting over... The main thing is not to think about the past or the future, the main thing is to just get on with now."

It was a snub for their long-time manager. For almost six years, Brian Epstein—affectionately known to the Beatle entourage as Eppy—had tried to be a guru to John, Paul, George and Ringo. He loved them and shared their fears and aspirations. At first, it had been his skill and business experience which had made them famous, but when the Beatles played their final gig in August 1966 they were far more than his boyish discoveries.

THOUGHTS WILL TRAVEL

On tour Epstein had always tried to make the schedule run smoothly; if there was a problem with transport, or accommodation, Brian would sort it out. Now it seemed as though he was an unnecessary fifth wheel. Brian had only ever wanted to share in their glory, but the Beatles

were tired of being Beatles; they just wanted to be themselves.

Epstein certainly made some serious business mistakes in the early days. Perhaps the costliest error was to seriously undervalue the worth of Beatle souvenirs in 1963. He had allowed 90% of all merchandise royalties to go to Seltaeb, the company that administered all Beatles licenses. His attempt to renegotiate the agreement in 1964 resulted in a successful three-year court battle, but by the time they had won, the Beatles' losses amounted to millions of dollars.

However, as Epstein's career continued he piled success upon success, not only with NEMS Enterprises but also with his new American company, Nemperor Artists. Yet his private life constantly undermined his public achievements—not that the public knew anything about his problems.

Since early adulthood Epstein had a led a secret, and at the time illegal, homosexual life, alternating between need and fear of discovery. He spent money, often lavishly, certainly unwisely, on pills, alcohol, rendezvous with rough young men and flamboyant spins of the roulette wheel. In August 1967, his contract with the Beatles was nearly at an end, and he knew that they no longer needed him.

At core his biggest heartache was John Lennon, whom he had adored almost from the first moment, and who had condescendingly put up with Epstein's unrequited love mopes in a manner probably not intended to be cruel, but which almost certainly was—John could be very mean in his wit.

> **"They weren't a business to Brian: they were a vocation, a mission in life. They were like a religion to him."**
> *Nat Weiss describing his friend, Brian Esptein*

Epstein's worries, and a deepening depression, drove him further into chemical dependency and on August 27 he was found dead in his home. The coroner announced the cause of death to be an accidental overdose of Carbitrol, which Epstein had been taking to help him sleep.

In Wales, the Maharishi told the Beatles not to be overwhelmed by grief but to remember Brian with fondness because "any thoughts we have of him, will travel to him wherever he is".

I Saw A Film Today, Oh Boy

Brian Epstein might have been an unlikely companion to the greatest rock band in the world, but his absence showed itself immediately in their next, and most lacklustre work, the misguided Beatles home-movie *Magical Mystery Tour*.

Paul's idea was to fill a brightly-coloured bus with different people, drive it around Devon and Cornwall for a week, and somehow make a film as they went along. Unfortunately, the Beatles' Midas touch turned horribly wrong. The 52-minute improvized story never got off the

The musical set-pieces weren't enough to rescue *Magical Mystery Tour*, but 'I Am The Walrus' got plenty of plays.

ground—throughout the mystery tour the only real action was happening off-camera, where the Beatles were constantly hampered by their lack of organization and by crowds of curious onlookers who followed them everywhere.

The few sequences which alleviated the boredom were the musical set-pieces, featuring six new songs including the catchy title track, the surreal classic 'I Am The Walrus'—which gave them another interesting promo "video" and kept that song playing the airwaves—and George Harrison's dazed and confused 'Blue Jay Way'. But the music wasn't enough to rescue it. BBC Television saved it up as a Christmas treat, broadcasting it on 26 December, 1967 to an eager young audience, who faithfully tried to like it. Next day newspaper critics tore it to shreds.

An American TV deal was cancelled on the strength of the British showing, although the music *was* released on an album in the US. Featuring the six new songs, plus the A- and B-sides of the band's 1967 singles: 'Hello Goodbye', 'Strawberry Fields', 'Penny Lane', 'Baby You're A Rich Man, and 'All You Need Is Love' it sold well but didn't cause a stir.

Coach of fools: the improvized *Magical Mystery Tour* turned into a creative disaster without Brian Epstein to keep the Beatles under control.

"'What we should have been filming was the chaos we caused."
Neil Aspinall, recalling the Magical Mystery Tour

their desertion of the others; the Lennons did better, they managed 11 weeks.

"We made a mistake," said John. "We're human. That's all." In the hope of restoring their winning streak, they announced the formation of a new enterprise—Apple Corps. "The aim of the company isn't a stack of gold teeth in the bank,"

> **"We only use one-tenth of our brains. Just think what we'd accomplish if we could tap that hidden part."**
> *Paul McCartney confessing to experimentation with LSD in 1967*

John explained at a press conference in New York, "we've done that bit. It's more of a trick to see if we can get artistic freedom within a business structure."

Like *Magical Mystery Tour*, Apple Corps was another naïve scheme with inevitably disastrous

Without Epstein's guidance, the collective Beatles' creativeness had turned to anarchy, and Paul McCartney was no Dick Lester behind the self-indulgent camera. A sense that they had created a mess drove another wedge between the Fab Four.

APPLE CORPSE

In 1968, the Beatles grew yet further apart. After a trip to India to study under the Maharishi, they returned to Britain, still with no sense of purpose and disenchanted with the holy leader. Ringo and Maureen could stand only 11 days of the spicy food and transcendental meditation before returning home making "no comment" about

After only eight months, the Apple Boutique on London's famous Baker Street was closed down and all the remaining stock given away.

results. It had begun in embryo in 1967 with the Apple Boutique in London's Baker Street. The shop—its exterior garishly painted in psychedelic style—sold "beautiful things for beautiful people" and was run by a radical but inept fashion collective, The Fool. Then John asked his old school friend Pete Shotton, now a Liverpool supermarket manager, to take an office above the boutique to run Apple Retail. The Apple empire

After a psychedelic facelift it reopened as Apple Corps, the Beatles' new creative banking emporium. The garish mural was so unpopular with residents it was later overpainted by local authority orders.

Pepperland and Blue Meanies: the Beatles turned into cartoon heroes for the animated movie, *Yellow Submarine*, but for London's "Blue Meanies", its premiere proved tough.

spiralled outward from there, quickly running out of their control and moving into bigger and more expensive premises.

In April 1968 the Beatles foolishly announced that they wanted to hear from novelists, artists, film-makers and performers. In the hands of friends like Pete Shotton and Neil Aspinall (their road manager turned Apple managing director) the group's money was wisely spent, but now there were many new faces in the plush Apple offices.

The Beatles expected to change the face of

commerce with one philanthropic swoop. They planned to give money to creative thinkers of all flavours, then sit back to receive the glory as their protégés achieved success. It didn't happen like that. According to John, the people who came to them were "bums". Apple Corps spread its funds far and wide, and yet created nothing

significant. In July 1968, the boutique went into liquidation, giving away all the remaining stock. From there, the whole business went into a steep decline, not much helped by the qualified success of the non-Apple *Yellow Submarine* project.

According to George Martin, the Beatles were loathe to become involved in the animated feature film. "The idea of being portrayed in cartoon form was basically abhorrent to them," he said, "but once it became a success, of

Japanese artist Yoko Ono was the only one who understood John Lennon's weird ways.

Yoko was constantly at John's ear, whispering advice

tured four original songs (studio out-takes which had failed to meet the band's strict standards) and a specially-written score by George Martin.

THE JAPANESE INFLUENCE

Despite Apple Corps, the mistake of *Magical Mystery Tour* and the non-Beatle *Yellow Submarine*, it was one individual who took the brunt of the blame for the band's disintegration. It was neither John, Paul, George nor Ringo, but a tiny, Japanese avant garde artist named Yoko Ono.

She first caught John's eye in 1966 at the Indica art gallery in London's fashionable West End, where she was presenting an exhibition titled *Unfinished Paintings And Objects*. For two years they kept in contact and John became more drawn to her. She was the first person he'd met who understood his "weird" ideas.

John had always felt different, but only as a Beatle could he express his unique emotions. Now there was a fiercely independent, wildly imaginative new force in his life, someone who believed in him not just as Paul McCartney's

course, they were delighted with it." The animation began development in 1966, but by the time of its premiere on July 17, 1968, it presented a dated picture of the happy-go-lucky Fab Four. Yet, for all its failings, it captured the spirit of the band where their own amateur film had failed.

The group went off to Pepperland to fight the Blue Meanies, singing songs and saving souls along the way. The Beatles had little to do with the actual making of the movie, which received only a limited theatrical release in the UK, and played to lacklustre audiences. However, it fea-

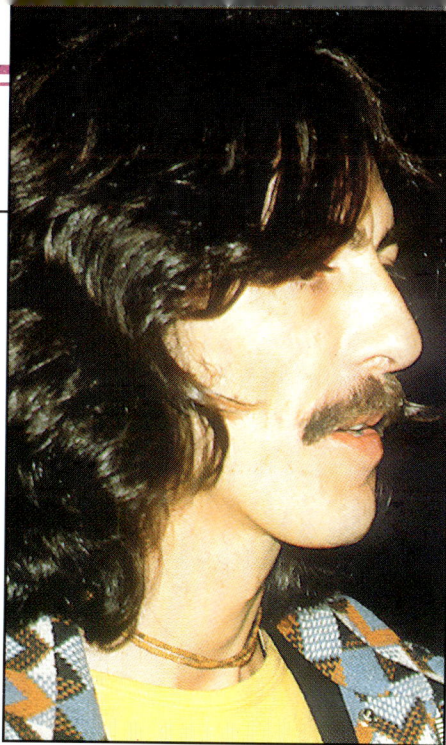

Weeping guitar: so far apart had the Beatles grown that George made his songs on The Beatles into solo projects.

copilot, but as an artist in his own right. John was swept away in her whirlwind of ideas, and in 1968 he realized that he'd found his true soul mate. Unfortunately, his good news was viewed askance by his old friends.

When the band returned to the studio to record new songs they'd written in India, Yoko Ono was ever-present, somehow violating their inner sanctum. Paul and George felt that her presence was an insult. Brian Epstein and George Martin, who had justly earned their respect, had never interfered with the Beatles' music, but Yoko was constantly at John's ear, whispering advice and criticizing their work.

Cynthia Lennon, who had always stood quietly in the shadow of her husband—and even concealed her existence from the public eye in the early days when it was considered unpolitic for a male pop idol to be married—was granted a divorce in November 1968. As a note of sympathy, Paul dedicated a song to John's estranged son, Julian Lennon. It's a song of encouragement for the times when life seems to be at its lowest ebb: 'Hey Jude'. Most pop singles in 1968 were no longer than three minutes so it was another challenge to the way things were when the Beatles released a single with a running time of over seven minutes.

George Martin pleaded to have the dead-weight tracks removed from *The Beatles* (or *The White Album*), but he wasn't listened to.

Because of its length, 'Hey Jude' was anathema to most radio stations, but 'Sgt. Pepper' had made it clear that pop songs no longer had to comply with their traditional constraints. The Beatles were proved right when 'Hey Jude' became their biggest-selling single of all.

ALL IN WHITE

Back in the studio, there was an icy atmosphere. Epstein was no longer there to guide them. Paul and John could no longer work together—Yoko's presence, intentionally or otherwise, had come down like a wall between them. George had developed into a prolific songwriter and was frustrated with his traditional quota of one or two songs per album. He brought in his friend Eric Clapton to play lead guitar on 'While My Guitar Gently Weeps', unambiguously turning the song into his solo project.

After five months of miserable work at the Abbey Road studios, Ringo was the one who snapped. Getting up from his drum kit he announced that he was just "not getting through", and went away to cool off for a week, leaving the remaining Beatles to record alone. (They completed the recording of 'Back In The USSR' with Paul as drummer.)

When Ringo returned, sessions continued until 30 songs of varying quality had been completed. There were some wonderful tracks: 'While My Guitar Gently Weeps' was George's finest, most mature song to date; Paul's 'Blackbird' was a beautiful ballad; and John's song in tribute to his mother, 'Julia', is a rare glimpse of a sentimental style more common to Paul. However, not all of the songs were such classics.

George Martin pleaded with them to scrap the dead weight—tracks like the throwaway Lennon lullaby, 'Good Night' (sung by Ringo), and the discordant, frankly meaningless eight-minute soundscape 'Revolution 9', created by John and Yoko. However, the Beatles were beyond compromise. Eschewing the blatant hippy symbolism of the *Sergeant Pepper* sleeve, the Beatles' first album on Apple Records was devoid of any association, political, musical or otherwise. It was plainly white, with only "The BEATLES"

Quiet shadow of her husband, Cynthia Lennon divorced John in November 1968.

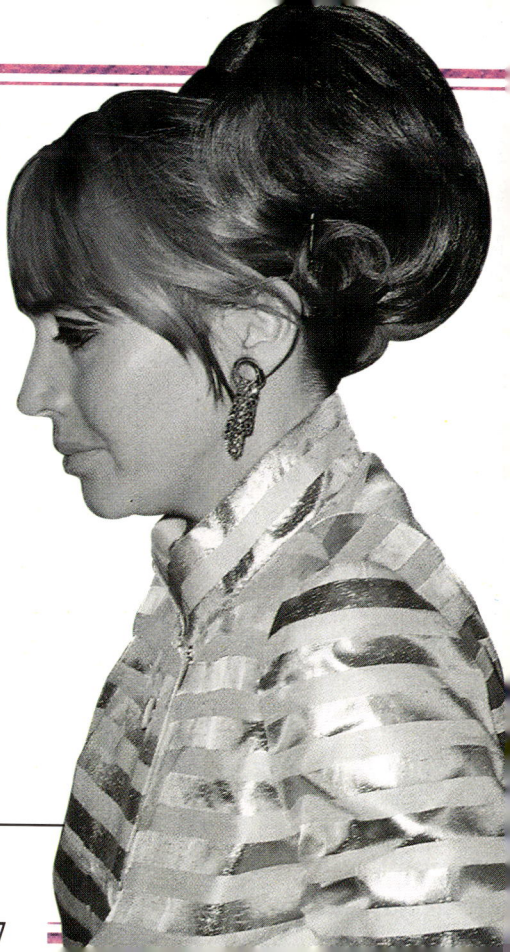

It wasn't the only Beatle-related release of the month. A week later out came John and Yoko's first experimental album, *Two Virgins*, with a controversial sleeve picturing the two lovers naked. By January, Paul seemed to be the only Beatle interested in keeping the band together. They met at Twickenham film studios, near London, with the idea of filming a TV special, featuring live performances of new songs—to get back to their roots. But the new material was not their best, and the resentments that had appeared during the last sessions were unabated.

APPLE OF DISCORD

What made things worse was the spectre of the crumbling Apple Corps looming over them. Apple Records had been a success—both 'Hey Jude' and *The White Album* were huge hits, and Beatle-produced records by the Black Dyke Mills Band and Mary Hopkin had both been well received. However, other Apple companies had not fared so well. Apple Films had no films in production, Apple Retail had never revived from the failure of the boutique… yet money continued to pour out of the coffers.

In the end, the footage shot at Twickenham was not destined to be used on TV. After a few

March 12, 1969: "The last Beatle bachelor marries!" screamed the world's headlines, as Paul married New Yorker Linda Eastman at Marylebone Register Office in London.

crookedly printed slightly off-centre. Just as it said nothing, it said it all. The album was released as a double-record set in November 1968 called simply *The Beatles*, but invariably known as *The White Album*.

Publicity pictures in 1969 still showed the Fab Four together—but in reality they were worlds apart from each other.

days, George became infuriated by Paul's steering and cajoling and walked out. In a meeting a few days later he threatened to quit the band unless Paul gave up the idea altogether of playing live. It was agreed that they would continue to play, but this time in the new Apple Studios (another disastrous project), for the filming of a documentary feature and studio album to be titled *Get Back*.

The Beatles were joined by pianist Billy Preston, an old friend from Hamburg who had met them while touring in Little Richard's band in 1962. At the end of January they were filmed jamming together on the roof of the Apple building in Savile Row, London. The 42-minute performance—not exactly a concert but certainly their last ever public appearance playing music together—was halted by police over problems with controlling the crowds below. The recording finished the next day, but *Get Back* was immediately abandoned. Not one Beatle had been happy with the sessions, and such was their apathy that they couldn't be bothered to do anything about it. Meanwhile, the Beatles' accountants had

resigned, and Apple desperately needed a top business troubleshooter to take over and rescue what was left.

Even here there was discord, with Paul trying to be business-like, while the others hovered between open animosity and apathy. In February 1969, after much argument between the four bewildered Beatles, Allen Klein, the accountancy genius who had made a fortune for the Rolling Stones, was appointed as the new manager.

CROSSING THE ROAD

In March, having split from Jane Asher six months earlier, Paul McCartney married New Yorker Linda Eastman, and a week later John Lennon married Yoko Ono. George and Ringo had both been married several years, and Ringo now had a second baby son. Both musically and emotionally they had less and less in common, yet in an attempt to bring back a glimmer of Beatles magic, Paul went to George Martin and asked him to produce an album for them "like the old days". And surprisingly, it worked.

They began in April with 'The Ballad Of John And Yoko', which subsequently appeared only as a single (and was their first ever stereo single release, reaching Number 1 in Britain and Number 8 in the USA). Recording continued with George's beautiful love song 'Something', but most of the work on what became called—suit-

A photographer by training, Linda was to have a lasting influence over Paul.

ably, because of everything they had achieved there—*Abbey Road*, took place between July 1–August 20, 1969—the last day that the four Beatles were in the EMI studios together.

The album cover, capturing for posterity the pedestrian crossing outside the EMI studios in St John's Wood, was another classic. It was the ultimate iconoclastic Beatle image: four superstars walking unharassed in the street, a simple pleasure which had long since been denied them.

Although it is less a band effort than their early work—indeed the second side is almost entirely a showcase for Paul's new songs—*Abbey Road* served as the final tribute to the talents of four Liverpool boys who had taken the sound of skiffle from a tiny club called The Cavern and turned it into a cultural revolution. George Harrison was beginning to demonstrate the unique talent which would manifest itself in the superb triple album set *All Things Must Pass* two years later. The meandering 'I Want You (She's So Heavy)' was Lennon at his best, typical of his wild disregard for musical conventions.

Most of all, Paul's new songs on side two were spine-tingling. The closing 'Golden Slumbers', 'Carry That Weight' and 'The End' closed the door on the psychedelic era and on

the Beatles' career with the words: "And in the end/The love you take/Is equal to the love/You make."

LET IT ALONE

Allen Klein soon realized he could never put Apple back on the rails. He started his new job with a series of swift and ruthless sackings. Financial problems continued throughout 1969, with the Beatles badgered by media mogul Lew Grade, whose Associated Television (ATV) company had bought up a share of Northern Songs. By the time *Abbey Road* was released, ATV had effectively gained the ownership of the Beatles' songs, for which their new manager secured them a massive cash payment.

Meanwhile, Klein sold the *Get Back* movie to United Artists, with American record producer Phil Spector brought in to try to revive shelved *Get Back* material. Spector sifted through 100 recorded songs spanning 24 hours of tape. The result was *Let It Be*, released finally in Britain on May 8, 1970, as a boxed set with an accompanying book. Two other Beatles' albums were tentatively planned from the same sessions—a collection of rerecorded oldies like 'Norwegian Wood' and 'Love Me Do', and also a rock'n'roll

1969: John and Yoko pleaded for peace from their travelling bridal bed—but there was to be no peace for the Beatles.

album of songs by other artists, from 'Blue Suede Shoes' to 'Tracks Of My Tears'. Sadly, those albums have never appeared—at least, not yet.

For *Let It Be*, the original, raw-sounding recordings were completely remixed by Spector, who overdubbed strings on 'Let It Be', 'I Me Mine', 'Across The Universe' and 'The Long And Winding Road', to which he also added a choir of 14 backing vocalists. The album is a patchy swansong, but beneath the swelling over-production there are some superb songs.

'Get Back' is a rockin' live track, which was released as yet another transatlantic chart-topper. It was also the only Beatles song to acknowledge a supporting musician, credited as "The Beatles with Billy Preston". 'The Long And Winding Road' became one of the best-loved of Paul's songs, with a meaning for everyone. Likewise, the message 'Let It Be' seemed particularly apt—now was not the time to think about the past; the new decade was full of hope for the future.

John's career as a solo artist was already burgeoning by 1970. His superb anthem, 'Give Peace A Chance', had been a worldwide hit in 1969, and the accompanying bed-ins had finally given him an identity—albeit a pretty kooky one, in his own write, so to speak. He'd even made his return to the stage with the Plastic Ono Band.

> **"This place has become a haven for drop-outs. The trouble is, some of our best friends are drop-outs."**
> *George Harrison on Apple Corps*

George had recorded an experimental solo album for Zapple Records (another Apple spin-off) and played a low-key tour as guitarist with Delaney & Bonnie. Ringo, for his part, seemed satisfied with a career as an actor, having recently appeared alongside Peter Sellers in *The Magic Christian*. But ironically it was the Beatle who had strived for nearly 18 months to keep them together who finally broke them up. When Paul released his aggressively-titled debut album, *McCartney*, on April 17, 1970, the Beatles story came to an end.

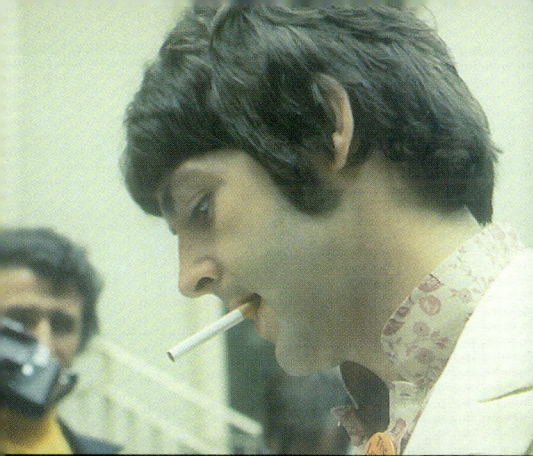

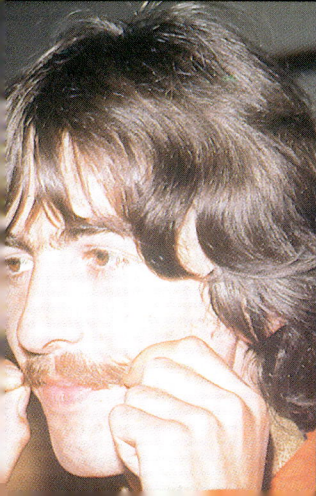

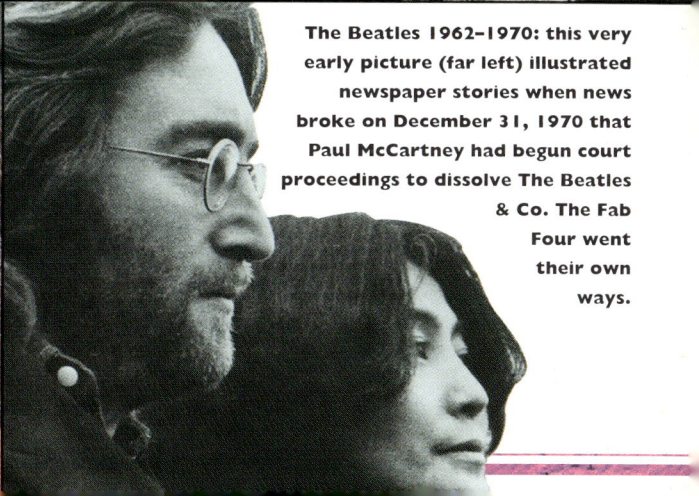

The Beatles 1962–1970: this very early picture (far left) illustrated newspaper stories when news broke on December 31, 1970 that Paul McCartney had begun court proceedings to dissolve The Beatles & Co. The Fab Four went their own ways.

AFTERMATH

The Beatles had ended, leaving tearful fans shocked and destitute. It was, however, simply unthinkable that the world's most successful band had broken up for good, and for many months after Paul made it official, fans everywhere were convinced the Beatles would get together again. But you only had to watch the documentary feature movie *Let It Be* to see the evidence, graphically detailed, of the chasms that had opened between the Fab Four. It was equally unthinkable that that was the end of John, Paul, George and Ringo—and of course, it wasn't.

John Lennon And The Plastic Ono Band, released in January 1971, established John and Yoko on the cutting edge of experimental music. Resulting from primal scream therapy, 'Mother' exorcised some of the demons of his past with an anguished howl, while 'God' proclaimed his self-determination with the line "I don't believe in Beatles... I just believe in me".

In 1972 he made his one and only solo live performance at a benefit concert in New York,

following it up with a seasonal classic UK Number 4 single, 'Happy Christmas (War Is Over)'. In 1974 he had his first solo Number 1 in the USA with 'Whatever Gets You Through The

> **"I thought we were the best group in the world. But play me those tracks today and I want to remake every one of them."**
> *John Lennon*

Night', and a year later returned to his teenage roots with an album of cover versions called *Rock'N'Roll*.

For the next six years he steered clear of the limelight—apart from the angst he caused among

---

"I don't believe in Beatles... I just believe in me": a new 1970 haircut for John as he and Yoko set out to become the cutting edge of experimental music.

Liverpudlians that their hero should select New York as his permanent home. John and Yoko returned in 1980 with the album *Double Fantasy*, released by Geffen Records, which received excellent reviews and topped the USA and UK charts. At the peak of his solo career, John had been hinting at a personal comeback world tour in a series of promotional interviews.

Then, on the evening of December 8, 1980 he returned to his home, the Dakota Building in New York, after visiting the Hit Factory recording studio. As he turned to answer a voice behind him calling out "Mr Lennon?", he was shot five times at close range by deranged fan Mark Chapman. He was rushed to hospital, but pronounced dead on arrival. His death shocked the world, truly, because despite his unique ability to irritate, people everywhere found that John Lennon had become an icon.

BAND ON THE RUN

Typically, Paul's post-Beatle career followed a far more commercial line than John's. He followed up his 1970 US Number 1, *McCartney*,

with the UK Number 1, *Ram*. Unlike John's obscure, alternative recordings, Paul continued writing tuneful pop songs with traditional appeal, consolidating his position in the charts for years to come. The peak of his commercialism was reached when he wrote and sang the title theme for the James Bond film *Live And Let Die*.

With his wife, Linda, he formed Wings, debuting with *Wings Wildlife* only six months after the release of his second solo album. Featuring the banned single 'Give Ireland Back To The Irish', written in response to the Belfast Bloody Sunday massacre, it was panned by the music press who turned against him until the best-selling *Band On The Run* was released in 1974.

In 1975 Wings embarked on a massive world tour, playing to more than two million people in 13 months. Having started from scratch with a new line-up and without the support of the media, Paul McCartney had proved his talent and widespread popularity as an individual rather than as a Beatle. In 1977 his single, 'Mull Of Kintyre', co-written with Denny Laine of Wings, topped the UK chart for nine weeks, deposing 'She Loves

You' as the biggest-selling UK single in chart history with more than 2.5 million copies sold.

In 1979 he was declared the most successful composer of all time, credited for 43 songs which had sold a million copies or more. With the Beatles, Wings, and as a solo artist he had sold 100 million albums and 100 million singles worldwide.

Paul's hits continued through the Eighties, including 'Ebony And Ivory'—a duet with Stevie Wonder—and 'Say, Say, Say' with Michael

animated film about Rupert the Bear realized a project he had long envisioned, and the video tape went on to be one of the year's best-sellers.

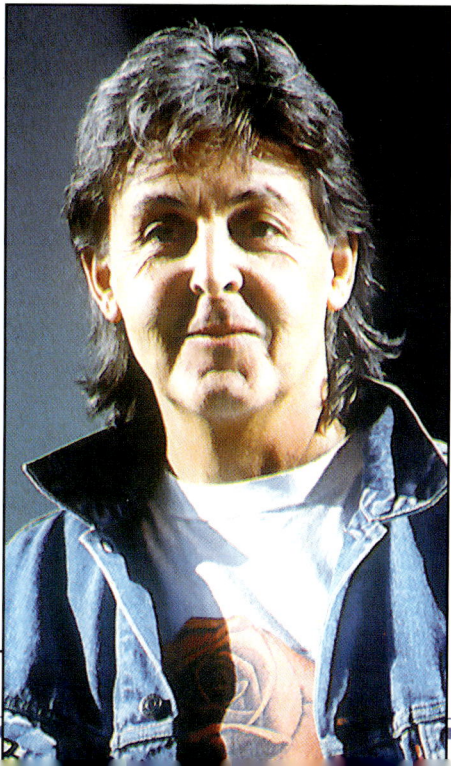

> **"I'm just the conservative of the four of us. Not compared with outside people. Compared to my family I'm a freak-out."**
> *Paul McCartney*

Jackson, both lifted from the highly successful *Pipes Of Peace* album. Although the film *Give My Regards To Broad Street* repeated the fiasco of *Magical Mystery Tour*, the soundtrack album was a UK Number 1 hit. His music for a short

Paul McCartney today—still going strong

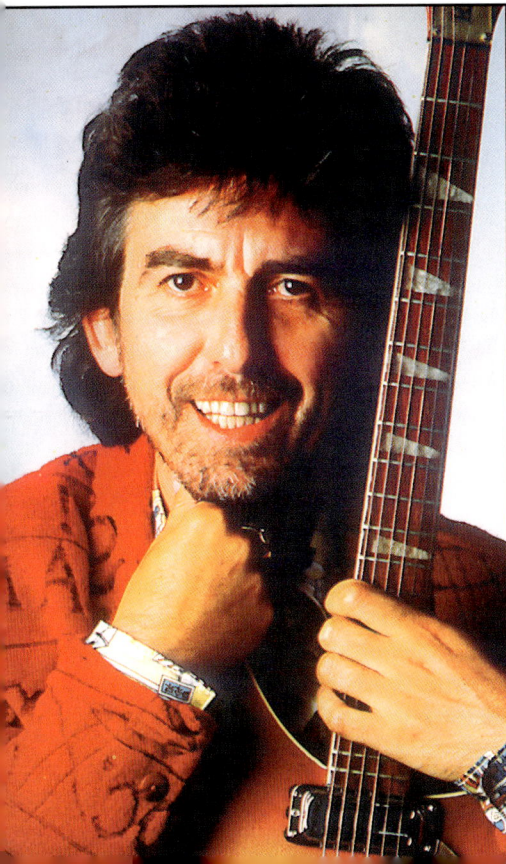

George became a successful film producer as well as a musician.

Like John before him, Paul recorded an album of rock'n'roll classics—initially for release only in the USSR—followed by his most accomplished solo album to date, *Flowers In The Dirt*, in 1989. This release heralded his return to the stage with a 46-week world tour playing 102 dates; and his concert appearances have continued into the Nineties. In 1993 he released a new studio album, *Off The Ground*, and an eclectic live album, *Paul Is Live*, featuring new tracks alongside oldies like 'Drive My Car', 'All My Loving' and 'Paperback Writer'.

HANDMADE

George didn't hang around, either, releasing the three-record set *All Things Must Pass* in December 1970. This was George Harrison's masterpiece, featuring support from musicians Eric Clapton, Ringo Starr, Billy Preston and Ginger Baker, and deservedly topped the US album chart. The single 'My Sweet Lord' topped the UK and US charts, and attained notoriety when George was sued by the publishers of the 1963 hit 'He's So Fine' by the Chiffons

George Harrison playing live.

In 1972, Harrison topped the UK chart again with another triple-album, *The Concert For Bangla Desh* (recorded at a charity benefit in August 1971), which was named Album Of The Year at the 15th Annual Grammy Awards. And in 1974 he formed his own record label, Dark Horse, releasing an album of the same name.

After a stressful period of uncertainty, his wife Pattie Boyd left him for his close friend Eric Clapton, but George bore no grudges and when Clapton married Boyd in 1979, George joined the nearest thing yet to a Beatles reunion when he

> **"I was always rather beastly to George."**
> *George Martin on George Harrison*

performed with Ringo Starr and Paul McCartney at the wedding reception. Besides, he'd already remarried, to Olivia Arias, in 1978.

Like Paul, George had caught the film bug, but proved more commercially astute with his choices, financing a series of mainstream successes at

for infringement of copyright. A US district court found against him and the publisher, Bright Tunes, was paid over US$500,000 (£250,000) in compensation.

relatively low budgets through his own Handmade Films company. Hits included the Monty Python film *Life Of Brian* and the fantasy adventure *Time Bandits*, directed by Terry Gilliam. However, he suffered a flop with *Shanghai Surprise*, starring Madonna and husband Sean Penn, which severely restricted the company's growth in 1986.

In 1987 he recorded his first solo album in five years, *Cloud Nine*, at his own home studio. It featured the US Number 1 single 'Got My Mind Set On You', which went on to be a worldwide hit, giving him a totally unexpected comeback. However, although he went on to participate in the phenomenal Traveling Wilburys with Roy Orbison, Bob Dylan and Tom Petty, he has since returned to his customary low profile.

NOT JUST A DRUMMER

Ringo stayed on safe ground, getting George Martin to produce his first solo outing, *Sentimental Journey*, an album of standards featuring Ringo's unique interpretations of tracks like 'Night and Day' and 'Bye Bye Blackbird'.

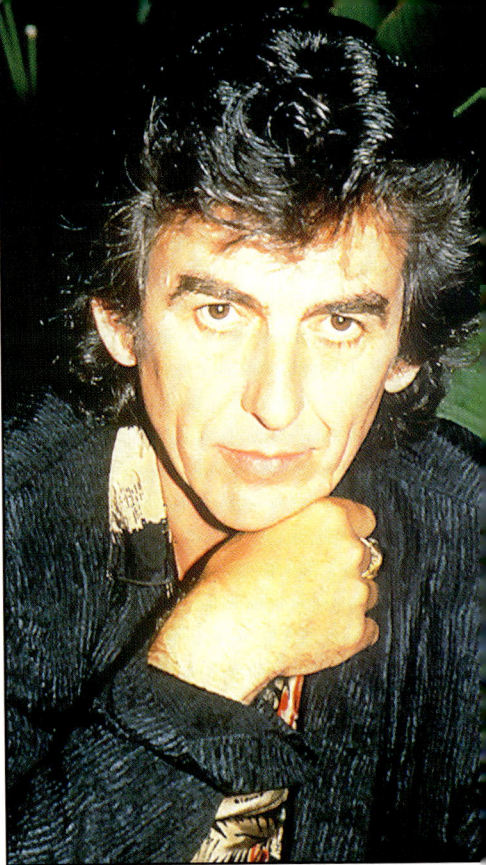

Ringo on The Tour For All Generations

He, too, juggled his musical ambitions with a film career, appearing in two movies in 1971, Frank Zappa's psychedelic *200 Motels* and the Italian spaghetti western, *Blindman*. He directed a concert movie starring T Rex and in 1973 starred with David Essex in the fictional rock biopic *That'll Be The Day*.

A second solo album, *Ringo*, featured contributions from both George Harrison and John Lennon, and the single, 'Photograph', went to Number 1 in the US. A cover of the old Johnny Burnette hit, 'You're Sixteen', also topped the Billboard chart. But over time Ringo's career drifted out of the spotlight. In the latter half of the Seventies he released several albums and singles, but with little success. *Ringo The 4th*, 1977,

reached only Number 162 in the US. A year later *Bad Boy*, a collection of cover versions, made Number 129.

In 1981 he remarried, to actress Barbara Bach, and became a grandfather in 1985. Ringo's career in broadcasting was boosted by the worldwide success of the British animated children's stories *Thomas The Tank Engine*, which he narrated. After a battle with alcoholism, he celebrated his first year of sobriety in 1989 with a comeback

> **"I don't have much to say, 'cause I'm the quiet Beatle."**
> *George Harrison on his induction to the Rock'n'Roll Hall Of Fame in 1988*

Ringo makes a comeback in 1989 after recovering from alcohol addiction.

concert tour. In June 1992 he released his first studio album for nine years, *Time Takes Time*, featuring the impressive single 'Weight Of The World', produced by Don Was.

Rumours that the Beatles would get together as a proper band again have been in continuous circulation, although without John Lennon the result would hardly be authentic. And would it ever be a satisfying event now that the survivors really are within striking distance of Paul McCartney's 'Sixty-Four'?

The Beatles' great repertoire of songs have remained fresh not only because they represent the most comprehensive collection of memorable pop music, but also because, like James Dean, they cannot be ruined by time and reappearance. Ater all, the Beatles have survived far longer than anyone in those heady days of 1964 could have ever anticipated—certainly longer than John Lennon expected. As he once said: "You can be big-headed and say 'Yeah, we're gonna last ten years', but as soon as you've said that you think, you know, we're lucky if we last three months."

"We're lucky if we last three months..."

CHRONOLOGY

1940 July 7: Richard Starkey born. October 9: John Lennon born.

1942 June 18: Paul McCartney born.

1943 February 25: George Harrison born.

1957 July: Paul sees John Lennon's band, The Quarrymen, perform in Woolton, Liverpool. He is invited to join the band a few days later.

1958 August: George Harrison, Paul's school friend, is recruited into the line-up.

1959 November: Under the name Johnny & The Moondogs, the group reaches the final heat of the TV Star Search auditions in Manchester.

1960 January: John's friend, 19-year-old Stuart Sutcliffe, wins an art school prize and spends his winnings on a bass guitar. He immediately joins the band. May: The Silver Beetles tour Scotland as the backing band to Johnny Gentle. They temporarily recruit 36-year-old Tommy Moore on drums. August: Promoter Allan Williams recruits drummer Pete Best (born 1941) and books the Beatles for a three month residency in Hamburg. October: Also working in Hamburg with Rory Storm & The Hurricanes, Richard Starkey (aka Ringo Starr) plays drums on an amateur recording of 'Summertime' featuring John, Paul & George. December: Return to Liverpool; the Beatles perform at Litherland Town Hall, Liverpool, greeted by an ecstatic crowd.

1961 February: The Beatles make their debut at The Cavern. March-July: More gigs in Hamburg. In August they are invited to play on Tony Sheridan's version of 'My Bonnie' in sessions for orchestra leader Bert Kaempfert. Stu Sutcliffe remains in Hamburg to live with his fiancée. November: Brian Epstein sees the Beatles play at The Cavern.

1962 January: The Beatles audition unsuccessfully for Decca Records. Brian Epstein becomes their manager and begins to clean up their scruffy image. March: They appear on radio for the first time on *Teenager's Turn*. April: On returning to Hamburg for another 48 nights, the Beatles find that Stu Sutcliffe has died. June: the Beatles record demos with George Martin at the EMI studios in Abbey Road, London. August: Drummer Pete Best is unceremoniously sacked in favour of Ringo Starr. John

Lennon marries Cynthia Powell. They separate in 1968. October: Release of debut single, 'Love Me Do', which slowly climbs the UK chart, reaching Number 17 in December.

1963 February: Second single, 'Please Please Me', reaches UK Number 1. May: Debut album, *Please Please Me*, goes to UK Number 1 and remains at the top until November. September: 'She Loves You' hits the UK singles Number 1 spot. It holds the record for best-selling UK single until replaced by Paul McCartney and Wings with 'Mull Of Kintyre' in 1977. November: The second album, *With The Beatles*, knocks their debut off the top of the UK album chart

1964 February: 'I Want To Hold Your Hand' becomes the group's debut US Number 1 single. A succession of Beatles singles monopolize the top spot for the next three months. Their debut tour begins

in Washington on February 11. April: For one week, the Beatles' singles 'Can't Buy Me Love', 'Twist And Shout', 'She Loves You', 'I Want To Hold Your Hand' and 'Please Please Me' hold the top five places on the Billboard chart. June: First world tour begins. July: Premiere of the movie *A Hard Day's Night*, directed by Dick (Richard) Lester August: Beatlemania grips America during their second national tour.

1965 July: Premiere of *Help!* August: Third USA tour; they meet Elvis Presley in California, and are disappointed. September: Debut of *The Beatles* cartoon series on US TV. A spin-off feature film will be premiered in July 1968. The Beatles are presented with the MBE by the Queen in the Great Throne Room at Buckingham Palace. December: *Rubber Soul* is a transitional album for the Beatles, as they try to leave behind their moptop image. They

play their final British tour dates.

1966 January: George Harrison marries Pattie Boyd. They separate in 1974. May: The Beatles' appearance at the NME Poll Winners' Party is their final British concert. July: On a tour of the Far East, they unintentionally slur the first lady of the Philippines and are forced to leave the islands in haste. An article in US teen magazine *Datebook* recounting John Lennon's opinion of modern Christianity creates media uproar. August: The final US tour begins at the International Amphitheater in Chicago and ends 17 days later with the last ever Beatles concert, at Candlestick Park, San Francisco, on August 29. Their seventh album, *Revolver*, is a landmark in the history of pop music.

1967 March: 'Penny Lane' c/w 'Strawberry Fields Forever' reaches the UK Number 2, the first Beatles single not to top the chart since 1962.

May: EMI announces that the Beatles have now sold more than 200 million records. June: Release of the Beatles' masterpiece, *Sgt. Pepper's Lonely Hearts Club Band*. The international satellite TV show *Our World* features the first performance of peace anthem 'All You Need Is Love', viewed by an audience of at least 200 million. August: While the Beatles attend a conference of the Spiritual Regeneration League in Bangor, Wales, manager Brian Epstein is found dead. November: Recording of the final Christmas Fan Club Record, 'Christmas Time Is Here Again' December: Disastrous movie *Magical Mystery Tour* premieres on British television.

1968 February: The Beatles study under the Maharishi Mahesh Yogi in India. May: In the USA John and Paul announce their intentions behind the ill-fated Apple Corps project. June: In London, the National Theatre launches a production based on John Lennon's book of nonsense poetry, *In His Own Write*. August: Ringo walks out during recording sessions at Abbey Road, but returns a few days later. Cynthia Lennon sues John Lennon for divorce, citing his adultery with Yoko Ono. December: Double album *The Beatles* (*The White Album*) is a collection of individual projects.

1969 January: Filming and recording for a project which Paul suggests will help them "get back" to their roots. After a performance on the rooftop of the Apple Corps office in Savile Row, London, the project is indefinitely shelved. February: Allen Klein is appointed the Beatles' manager. March: Paul McCartney marries Linda Eastman. John Lennon marries Yoko Ono, staging a "bed-in" for peace in an Amsterdam hotel. June: 'The Ballad Of John And Yoko' is the band's first ever stereo single, and their final Number 1. August: The Beatles record together at Abbey Road for the last time. September: Release of *Abbey Road*, the last recorded Beatles album.

1970 April: Paul releases his debut solo album, *McCartney*, announcing the Beatles split officially. John is already recording with the Plastic Ono Band, and George has released an experimental solo LP. Ringo releases his George Martin-produced album *Sentimental Journey*. May: The *Get Back* project, remixed by Phil Spector, is released as *Let It Be*.

1979 Summer: Paul, George and Ringo perform together again, on the occasion of Eric Clapton's wedding to George's ex-wife, Pattie Boyd.

1980 December 8: John Winston Lennon dies in New York after being shot five times by disturbed fan Mark Chapman.

DISCOGRAPHY

SINGLES

Month Of Release	Title	Top UK Chart Position	Top US Chart Position
Oct 1962	Love Me Do	17	1
Jan 1963	Please Please Me	1	3
Apr 1963	From Me To You	1	116
Jun 1963	My Bonnie	48	
Aug 1963	She Loves You	1	1
Nov 1963	I Want To Hold Your Hand	1	1
Mar 1964	Twist & Shout *		1
Mar 1964	Can't Buy Me Love	1	1
Mar 1964	Do You Want To Know A Secret *	2	
May 1964	Sie Liebt Dich (German Version Of 'She Loves You')	/	97
Jun 1964	Ain't She Sweet	29	19
Jul 1964	A Hard Day's Night	1	1
Jul 1964	I'll Cry Instead **		25
Jul 1964	And I Love Her ***		12
Aug 1964	Matchbox #		17
Nov 1964	I Feel Fine	1	1
Feb 1965	Eight Days A Week ##		1
Apr 1965	Ticket To Ride	1	1
Jul 1965	Help!	1	1
Sep 1965	Yesterday ###		1
Dec 1965	We Can Work It Out/Day Tripper	1	1
Feb 1966	Nowhere Man +		3
Jun 1966	Paperback Writer	1	1
Aug 1966	Eleanor Rigby/Yellow Submarine	1	2
Feb 1967	Strawberry Fields Forever/ Penny Lane	2	1
Jul 1967	All You Need Is Love	1	1
Nov 1967	Hello, Goodbye	1	1
Dec 1967	Magical Mystery Tour Double EP ++	2	
Mar 1968	Lady Madonna	1	4
Aug 1968	Hey Jude	1	1
Apr 1969	Get Back	1	1
May 1969	The Ballad Of John & Yoko	1	8
Oct 1969	Something	4	1
Mar 1970	Let It Be	2	1
May 1970	The Long And Winding Road		1

* In the UK 'Twist And Shout' and 'Do You Want To Know A Secret' were released on an EP with 'A Taste Of Honey' and 'There's A Place'. It went to Number 1 in the EP chart.
** In the UK 'I'll Cry Instead' was released on an EP featuring 'Any Time At All', 'Things We Said Today' and 'When I Get Home'. It reached Number 8 in the EP chart.

*** In the UK 'And I Love Her' was released on an EP with 'I Should Have Known Better', 'If I Fell' and 'Tell Me Why'. It went to Number 1 in the EP chart.
\# In the UK 'Matchbox' was released on an EP which also featured:
'Long Tall Sally', 'I Call Your Name' and 'Slow Down'. It went to Number 1 on the EP chart.
\#\# In the UK 'Eight Days A Week' was released on an EP featuring:
'No Reply', 'I'm A Loser' and 'Rock & Roll Music'. It reached Number 1 on the EP chart.

\#\#\# In the UK 'Yesterday' was released on an EP featuring: 'Act Naturally', 'You Like Me Too Much' and 'It's Only Love' It reached Number 1 on the EP chart.
\+ In the UK 'Nowhere Man' was released on an EP featuring: 'Drive My Car', 'Michelle' and 'You Won't See Me'. It reached Number 4 in the EP chart. The separate EP chart was not published in the UK after November 1967.
\+\+ In the USA the tracks from the 'Magical Mystery Tour' double EP were available only on the album *Magical Mystery Tour*.

UK ALBUMS

Month Of Release	Title	Top Chart Position
Mar 1963	Please Please Me	1
Nov 1963	With The Beatles	1
Jul 1964	A Hard Day's Night	1
Dec 1964	Beatles For Sale	1
Aug 1965	Help!	1
Dec 1965	Rubber Soul	1
Aug 1966	Revolver	1
Dec 1966	A Collection Of Beatles Oldies	4
Jun 1967	Sgt. Pepper's Lonely Hearts Club Band	1
Nov 1967	Magical Mystery Tour (US Import Only)	31
Nov 1968	The Beatles (White Album)	1
Jan 1969	Yellow Submarine	4
Sep 1969	Abbey Road	1
May 1970	Let It Be	1

US ALBUMS

Month	Title	Top
Jan 1964	Meet The Beatles!	1
Jul 1963–Re-released Jan 1964	Introducing… The Beatles	2
Apr 1964	The Beatles With Tony Sheridan And Their Guests	68
Apr 1964	Jolly What! The Beatles And Frank Ifield	104
Apr 1964	The Beatles' Second Album	1
Jun 1964	A Hard Day's Night	1
Jul 1964	Something New	2
Oct 1964	The Beatles vs The Four Seasons	142
Nov 1964	The Beatles Story	7
Dec 1964	Songs, Pictures & Stories Of The Fabulous Beatles	63
Dec 1964	Beatles '65	1
Mar 1965	The Early Beatles	43
Jun 1965	Beatles VI	1
Aug 1965	Help!	1
Dec 1965	Rubber Soul	1
Jun 1966	'Yesterday'…And Today	1
Aug 1966	Revolver	1
Jun 1967	Sgt. Pepper's Lonely Hearts Club Band	1
Nov 1967	Magical Mystery Tour	1
Nov 1968	The Beatles (White Album)	1
Jan 1969	Yellow Submarine	2
Oct 1969	Abbey Road	1
Feb 1970	Hey Jude	2
May 1970	Let It Be	1

ALBUMS

(CD catalogue numbers)
Please note, CD numbers
are subject to periodic
change and revision

PLEASE PLEASE ME

UK: Parlophone
CDP 746 435 2
US: EMI US C2-46435-2
Producer: George Martin
Release Date: April, 1963

Side 1

I Saw Her Standing There
(McCartney-Lennon)
Misery
(McCartney-Lennon)
Anna (Go To Him)
(Arthur Alexander)
Chains
(Goffin-King)
Boys
(Dixon-Farrell)
Ask Me Why
(McCartney-Lennon)
Please Please Me
(McCartney-Lennon)

Side 2

Love Me Do
(McCartney-Lennon)
P.S. I Love You

(McCartney-Lennon)
Baby It's You
(David-Williams
Bacharach)
Do You Want To
Know A Secret
(McCartney-Lennon)
A Taste Of Honey
(Scott-Marlow)
There's A Place
(McCartney-Lennon)
Twist And Shout
Medley-Russell)

WITH THE BEATLES

UK: Parlophone
CDP 746 436 2
US: Capitol C2-46436-2
Producer: George Martin
Release Date: November
22, 1963

Side 1

It Won't Be Long
(Lennon-McCartney)
All I've Got To Do
(Lennon-McCartney)
All My Loving
(Lennon-McCartney)
Don't Bother Me
(George Harrison)
Little Child
(Lennon-McCartney)

Till There Was You
(Meredith Wilson)
Please Mister Postman
(Holland)

Side 2

Roll Over Beethoven
(Chuck Berry)
Hold Me Tight
(Lennon-McCartney)
You Really Got A Hold
On Me
(Smokey Robinson)
I Wanna Be Your Man
(Lennon-McCartney)
Devil In Her Heart
(Drapkin)
Not A Second Time
(Lennon-McCartney)
Money
(Bradford-Gordy)

A HARD DAY'S
NIGHT

UK: Parlophone
CDP 746 437 2
US: Capitol C2-46437-2
Producer: George Martin
Release Date: July 10,
1964

Side 1

A Hard Day's Night

I Should Have Known
Better
If I Fell
I'm Happy Just To
Dance With You
And I Love Her
Tell Me Why
Can't Buy Me Love

Side 2

Any Time At All
I'll Cry Instead
Things We Said Today
When I Get Home
You Can't Do That
I'll Be Back

All titles composed by
John Lennon and Paul
McCartney

Side-1 titles are all from
the film, those on Side-2
are not

SOMETHING NEW

UK: Not advised
US: Not advised
Producers: George
Martin (UK) and Dave
Dexter (US)
Release Date: July 20,
1964

Side 1

I'll Cry Instead
(Lennon-McCartney)
Things We Said Today
(Lennon-McCartney)
Any Time At All
(Lennon-McCartney)
When I Get Home
(Lennon-McCartney)
Slow Down
(Larry Williams)
Matchbox
(Carl Perkins)

Side 2

Tell Me Why
(Lennon-McCartney)
And I Love Her
(Lennon-McCartney)
I'm Happy Just To Dance
With You
(Lennon-McCartney)
If I Fell
(Lennon-McCartney)
Komm, Gib Mir
Deine Hand
(Lennon-McCartney)

'Komm, Gib Mir Deine
Hand' is the German
language version of 'I
Want To Hold Your
Hand'

BEATLES FOR SALE

UK: Parlophone
CDP 746 438 2
US: Capitol C2-46438-2
Producer: George Martin
Release Date: November
27, 1964

Side 1

No Reply
(Lennon-McCartney)
I'm A Loser
(Lennon-McCartney)
Baby's In Black
(Lennon-McCartney)
Rock And Roll Music
(Chuck Berry)
I'll Follow The Sun
(Lennon-McCartney)
Mr. Moonlight
(Johnson)
Kansas City
(Lieber-Stoller)

Side 2

Eight Days A Week
(Lennon-McCartney)
Words Of Love
(Buddy Holly)
Honey Don't
(Carl Perkins)
Every Little Thing
(Lennon-McCartney)

I Don't Want To Spoil
The Party
(Lennon-McCartney)
What You're Doing
(Lennon-McCartney)
Everybody's Trying To
Be My Baby
(Carl Perkins)

HELP!

UK: Parlophone
CDP 746 439 2
US: Capitol C2-46439-2
Producer: George Martin
Release Date: August, 1965

Side 1

Help!
Lennon-McCartney)
The Night Before
(Lennon-McCartney)
You've Got To Hide Your
Love Away
(Lennon-McCartney)
I Need You
(George Harrison)
Another Girl
(Lennon-McCartney)
You're Going To Lose
That Girl
(Lennon-McCartney)
Ticket To Ride
(Lennon-McCartney)

Side 2

Act Naturally
(Morrison-Russell)
It's Only Love
(Lennon-McCartney)
You Like Me Too Much
(George Harrison)
Tell Me What You See
(Lennon-McCartney)
I've Just Seen A Face
(Lennon-McCartney)
Yesterday
(Lennon-McCartney)
Dizzy Miss Lizzy
(Larry Williams)

Songs on Side 1 are from
the film; those on Side 2
are not.

RUBBER SOUL

UK: Parlophone
CDP 746 440 2
US: Capitol C2-46440-2
Producer: George Martin
Release Date: December
3, 1965

Side 1

Drive My Car
Norwegian Wood
You Won't See Me
Nowhere Man

Think For Yourself (*)
The Word
Michelle

Side 2
What Goes On
Girl
I'm Looking Through You
In My Life
Wait
If I Needed Someone (*)
Run For Your Life

All titles composed by
Lennon-McCartney,
except: (*) George
Harrison

REVOLVER
UK: Parlophone
CDP 746 441 2
US: Capitol C2-46441-2
Producer: George Martin
Release Date: August 5,
1966

Side 1
Eleanor Rigby
Taxman (*)
I'm Only Sleeping
Love You To (*)
Here, There And
Everywhere

Yellow Submarine
She Said She Said

Side 2
Good Day Sunshine
And Your Bird Can Sing
For No One
Doctor Robert
I Want To Tell You
Got To Get You Into
My Life
Tomorrow Never Knows

All titles by Lennon-
McCartney, except: (*)
George Harrison

A COLLECTION OF BEATLES OLDIES BUT GOLDIES
UK: Not advised
US: Not advised
Producer: George Martin
Release Date: November
1966

Side 1
She Loves You   1963
From Me To You   1963
We Can Work It Out 1965
Help!   1965
Michelle   1965
Yesterday   1965

I Feel Fine   1964
Yellow Submarine   1966

Side 2
Can't Buy Me Love   1964
Bad Boy   1965
Day Tripper   1965
A Hard Day's Night 1964
Ticket To Ride   1965
Paperback Writer   1966
Eleanor Rigby   1966
Want To Hold
Your Hand   1963

SGT. PEPPER'S LONELY HEARTS CLUB BAND
UK: Parlophone
CDPEPPER 1
US: Capitol C2-46442-2
Producer: George Martin
Release Date: June 1,
1967

Side 1
Sgt. Pepper's
Lonely Hearts Club Band
With A Little Help From
My Friends
Lucy In The Sky
With Diamonds
Getting Better
Fixing A Hole

She's Leaving Home
Being For The Benefit Of
Mr Kite

Side 2
Within You Without
You (*)
When I'm Sixty-Four
Lovely Rita
Good Morning Good
Morning
Sgt. Pepper's Lonely
Hearts Club Band
A Day In The Life

All titles by Lennon-
McCartney, except: (*)
George Harrison.

THE BEATLES
(The White Album)
UK: CD set Parlophone
CDS 746 443 8
US: Capitol C2-46443-2
Producer: George Martin
Release Date: November,
1968

Record 1: Side 1
Back In The USSR
Dear Prudence
Glass Onion
Ob-La-Di, Ob-La-Da

Wild Honey Pie
The Continuing Story of
Buffalo Bill
While My Guitar Gently
Weeps (*)
Happiness Is A
Warm Gun
Julia

Record 1: Side 2
Martha My Dear
I'm So Tired
Blackbird
Piggies (*)
Rocky Raccoon
Don't Pass Me By (+)
I Will

Record 2: Side 3
Birthday
Yer Blues
Mother Nature's Son
Everybody's Got
Something To Hide
Sexy Sadie
Helter Skelter
Long Long Long (*)

Record 2: Side 4
Revolution 1
Honey Pie
Savoy Truffle (*)
Cry Baby Cry

Revolution 9
Good Night

All titles by Lennon-
McCartney, except: (*)
George Harrison and (+)
Richard Starkey

YELLOW SUBMARINE
UK: Parlophone
CDPCS 7070
US: Capitol C2-46445-2
Producer: George Martin
Release Date: December,
1968

Side 1
Yellow Submarine
Only A Northern Song
All Together Now
Hey, Bulldog
It's All Too Much
All You Need Is Love
Yellow Submarine In
Pepperland

Side 2
Pepperland
Sea Of Time
Sea Of Holes
Sea Of Monsters
March Of The Meanies
Pepperland Laid Waste

Side-2 consists entirely of
instrumentals, performed
by the George Martin
orchestra.

ABBEY ROAD
UK: Parlophone
CDP 746 446 2
US: Capitol C2-46446-2
Producer: George Martin
Release Date: September
26, 1969

Side 1
Come Together
Something (*)
Maxwell's Silver
Hammer
Sun King
Mean Mr Mustard
Octopus's Garden (+)
I Want You (She's So
Heavy)
Carry That Weight
Her Majesty

Side 2
Here Comes The Sun (*)
Because
You Never Give Me
Your Money
Oh! Darling
Polythene Pam

She Came In Thru The
Bathroom Window
Golden Slumbers
The End

All songs by Lennon-
McCartney, except: (*)
George Harrison and (+)
Richard Starkey
'Her Majesty' was not
listed on the cover of
the original issue of the
LP, although it did
appear on the record
label

LET IT BE
UK: Parlophone
CDP 746 447 2
US: Capitol C2-46447-2
Producers: George
Martin, Glyn Johns,
Phil Spector
Release Date: May 8,
1970

Side 1
Two Of Us
Dig A Pony
Across The Universe
I Me Mine (*)
Dig It (#)
Let It Be

Side 2
I've Got A Feeling
One After 909
The Long And Winding
Road
For You Blue (*)
Maggie Mae (traditional)

All songs by Lennon-
McCartney, except: (*)
George Harrison, (+)
Richard Starkey, (#)
Lennon-McCartney-
Starkey-Harrison
'Maggie Mae' arranged
by Lennon-McCartney

AFTER THE SPLIT:
Some CD reissues

The Ultimate Box Set
UK: Parlophone
CDS 791 302 2
US: Capitol BBX2-
91302-2

CD Singles Collection
UK: Parlophone
CDBSCP 1
US: Not advised

1962-1966
UK: Parlophone

CDPCSP 7231
US: Capitol 97036

1967-1970
UK: Parlophone
CDPCSP 7241
US: Capitol 97039

EXTENDED PLAYS
Original Issues with Dates
This chart lists all original British titles and issue
dates up until 1974.

Title	Released
The BeatlesS Hits	Sep, 1963
Twist And Shout	Sep, 1963
The Beatles #1	Nov, 1963
All My Loving	7 Feb, 1964
Long Tall Sally	19 Jun, 1964
A Hard Day's Night #1	4 Nov, 1964
A Hard Day's Night #2	6 Nov, 1964
Beatles For Sale #1	196 Apr, 1965
Beatles For Sale #2	4 Jun, 1965
Beatles Million Sellers	5 Dec, 1965
Yesterday	4 Mar, 1966
Nowhere Man	8 Jul, 1966
Magical Mystery Tour [double EP]	Dec, 1967

American Issues and Dates
This chart lists all American issues of Beatles EPs and
issue dates (when known) until, 1970

TITLE	RELEASED
Misery/A Taste of Honey/Anna/	
Ask Me Why—Roll Over Beethoven/	
All My Loving/This Boy/Please	
Mr. Postman	11 May, 1964
Honey Don't/I'm A Loser/	
Mr. Moonlight/Everybody's Trying	
To Be My Baby	1 Feb, 1965

INDEX

PICTURE ACKNOWLEDGMENTS

Photographs reproduced by kind permission of **Hulton Deutsch Collection**/©Apple Corps; **London Features International**; **Pictorial Press**/Tony Gale; **Redferns**/ Glenn A. Baker,/Mick Hutson,/Astrid Kirchherr,/Susan Moore,/Petra Niemeier,/David Redfern,/Rick Richards,/S&G,/Anne Stern,/Vollmer; Front cover picture: London Features International